THE *Golden* GATE

THE Golden GATE

SUKEY GROSS

MENUCHA PUBLISHERS

Menucha Publishers, Inc.

First published 1989

© 1989, 2023 by Sukey Gross

ISBN 978-1-61465-484-1

Library of Congress Control Number: 2022946288

Published and distributed by:

Menucha Publishers, Inc.

1235 38th Street

Brooklyn, NY 11218

Tel/Fax: 718-232-0856

www.menuchapublishers.com

sales@menuchapublishers.com

Printed in Israel

To my parents,
Moshe Mordechai, *z"l,* **and Chana,** *a"h,* **Stavsky**

And to my in-laws,
Moshe, *z"l,* **and Rivkah,** *a"h,* **Gross**

And, *ybl"c,* to my mother-in-law,
Rochelle Gross

And to my dear husband,
Meir,
whose focus on Torah as the true *derech Hashem*
could not be matched

CONTENTS

1

A MYSTERIOUS FOLLOWER

Don't turn around," Sara said, "but I'm sure there's someone following us!"

Of course, when someone tells you not to turn around, your reaction is to do the exact opposite. So before Sara's words were even floating in the air, I turned around to take a brief look. She was right. There *was* someone following us.

He was Asian, skinny and slight. It was just the type of situation you read about in books, the kind you're sure the person following you is a spy.

"When did you first notice him?" I asked Sara.

"Well," she answered, thinking out loud. "This day has been very busy and exciting, what with going shopping in New York City and having your father let us tag along while he was having his meetings..."

Sara's voice trailed off as her eyes clouded up in her efforts to remember.

I was becoming a little frightened, but then, I always tend to be a scaredy cat. I tried to put on a brave front.

"Aw, come on," I said to Sara. "Don't you think my father would have noticed if someone was following us around?"

Sara looked at me with a puzzled frown on her face.

"That's just what I don't understand," she said. "If that man was really following us, we *should* have noticed him before."

I nodded my head in agreement and smiled. "Well, then," I answered. "You've answered your own question. The man can't be following us, 'cause for sure we would have noticed him before my father put us on the Pineville bus in Port Authority."

All of a sudden, Sara's eyes began to sparkle, and her face brightened as if the sun had emerged from behind a rain cloud.

"Why, that's just it," she exclaimed. "You've got it!"

"I've got what?" I asked hesitantly, afraid to find out the answer.

"We would never have discovered the Asian man following us in New York City," she explained in a patient tone of voice, "because New York City is *full* of Asian people.

"Besides which," Sara reminded me. "One of your father's meetings was in Chinatown."

I began to nod my head as I understood Sara's train of thought.

"Yet when we got to Pineville, an Asian following us would surely stick out," I concluded Sara's thoughts.

"Let's see if he really is following us. Let's test him out. First we'll slow down, and then we'll walk a little faster," Sara suggested. "Then we'll surely know if he's really following us, or if this whole scenario is just a funny coincidence."

I was ready to try anything to prove to Sara that her theory of someone following us was just her overactive imagination looking for excitement. I really doubted the person would find our walk very interesting. Sara, though, was always intent on veiling every action in mystery and excitement.

We turned the corner onto Oaktree Lane. Oaktree Lane is the main street of Pineville. That's where all the stores are located, and it's the busiest part of town.

The Asian man followed.

Trying to appear nonchalant, we walked into Yocheved-Yehudis, the local clothing store in town. We figured the man would have nothing to do with children's clothing. We were right. He didn't follow.

We stayed in the store for about fifteen minutes, looking at the new spring dresses on display. When we assumed the coast was clear, we ventured out of the store.

"See," I said to Sara, letting out a deep sigh of relief. "See, he wasn't following us. He didn't come into the store, and he's not waiting outside the store."

"Oh, yeah?" Sara questioned triumphantly. "Don't look in front of the barber shop, but there he is!"

Of course, I turned around to look, and Sara was right. The same man was standing in front of the barber shop, leaning against the window, seeming oblivious to our comings and goings.

"Quick!" Sara said. "There's a group of eighth graders coming down the street. Let's see if we can blend in with them."

Sara's words were like a command. As soon as the group approached us, we mingled with them. When we reached Marigold Road, the street where I live, both of us discreetly said goodbye to the eighth graders. We hurriedly continued down my block. When we reached my house, we both turned around and searched the street behind us. The man had gone.

"We lost him," Sara said with a sigh. She sounded a little disappointed.

"I hate to ruin your mystery," I said to her. "But I doubt he was really following us."

We slowly walked into my house, each absorbed in her own thoughts.

Sara Goodman loves a mystery. She's an effervescent bubble of boundless energy. She looks like a blonde pixie with freckles on her nose. She's always excitedly planning new adventures.

I'm just the opposite. My name is Bracha Friedman. I'm also short, although I am beginning to describe myself as petite. I have long brown hair that I wear in a ponytail.

I'm very quiet. I don't like having people look at me, and I blush outrageously when I'm the center of attention. That's why I'm glad Sara and I are such good friends. Sara tends to pull the attention away from me, and I can easily sit on the sidelines and shyly observe the goings-on.

"Hi, I'm home," I called out loud as Sara and I entered the house.

I heard music coming from the stereo in the living room, and Sara and I followed the sounds. My older brother Sruly was standing on top of a ladder taking out *sefarim* from the bookcase.

"Well, it's about time you came home from your shopping trip. Did you buy out the store? You know it's erev Pesach, and Mom needs as much help as possible."

My brothers tend to be a little bossy at times, but I have finally learned to ignore them. Ever since they started dorming at out-of-town yeshivos, I've learned that most of the time they are just teasing me.

"Hey, he's out there!" Sara exclaimed as she moved the curtain at the living room window ever so slightly so she could look outside.

I quickly rushed to her side and also peeked out of the window.

"You're right," I said a little nervously. "He was following us. I wonder why."

"Shh." Sara took me by the hand and signaled me to keep quiet. "We don't want your brother to get involved."

"Why not?" I asked. "I'm beginning to get frightened. After all, he followed us to *my* house."

"But *why* did he follow us?" Sara questioned. "Let's go up to your room and think about it. We have to figure this thing out."

I agreed to Sara's suggestion, and we went upstairs. I flopped down on my bed. Sara made herself comfortable on the carpet. She pulled up her knees, crossed her arms on top and rested her chin on her arms.

"Did we say anything on the bus that would interest that man?" she mused.

"I don't know," I admitted softly. "All we talked about was the bar mitzvah my parents are going to."

"What did you say about the bar mitzvah that would interest a stranger?" Sara asked further.

"Nothing I could imagine." I tried to remember our conversation on the bus. "All I remember saying was that my parents are invited to a cousin's bar mitzvah in San Francisco."

"No," Sara said decisively. "The bar mitzvah talk wouldn't interest anyone except us. Maybe..."

Sara has this uncomfortable habit of beginning a sentence and not quite finishing it.

"Maybe what?" I questioned my friend, figuratively tapping my toe, impatiently waiting for her expected outlandish answer.

Sara looked me in the eye, kind of gauging the amount of imaginative baloney I would accept.

"Maybe," she continued, "the Asian has been following us since Chinatown."

Sara paused for a moment to collect her thoughts. "And maybe," she continued, "this whole mystery has something to do with your father's meetings today."

I began to laugh at the ridiculousness of Sara's conclusions.

"And just maybe," I began to tease her, "my father was meeting a band of jewel thieves and he's purchasing stolen jewelry so he could resell it."

Sara smiled sheepishly.

"Well," she answered laughingly. "I wouldn't exactly go to that extreme."

Sara quickly raised herself from the floor (Sara always does things quickly), and peeked out of the window.

"He's still standing across the street," she said. "Maybe we should tell your mother."

I peeked out the window, and sure enough, the man was still standing there. As we watched, though, a strange scene began to unfold in front of our eyes.

First, let me explain something. We'd been referring to the Asian as a man. Yet even as we caught fleeting glances of him following us, we realized he was a lot younger than a grown-up man. As a matter of fact, he looked just about our age. Maybe that's why Sara wasn't too frightened, and rather saw the adventurous lining in his actions.

The guy was standing in the shadows of the budding trees across the street. It was beginning to darken outside as the sun was setting. He seemed to be both watching our house and keeping an eye on the street.

As we peered out of the window, we saw two pairs of youths walking toward him from opposite directions of the street. The young Asian seemed confused. The approaching youths were marching forward at a slow but steady pace. They seemed to realize that their victim, who'd been following us, was theirs for the taking.

The young Asian guy seemed cornered. Even though he'd been following us, I began to wish he'd be able to escape. I wondered if I should open the window and call to him and help him. But I was frozen to the spot.

Suddenly there was a screech of brakes. A dark car turned the corner at high speed and didn't quite stop in front of the Asian. The door was thrust open, and he leaped inside.

The two pairs of youths began to run toward the car, trying to prevent the escape of the Asian guy. They were too late, though, and reached the empty spot where he'd been standing, only to find the dust beginning to settle.

The four youths stood together in the same shadow of the tree and seemed to confer for a minute or two. Suddenly, all four turned around and faced my house. I found myself frozen to the spot and jumped as Sara shut the blind suddenly in my face.

But it wasn't before my eyes had encountered the hard, cold stare of four pairs of eyes looking straight at me.

Quickly, Sara and I ran down the stairs and entered the kitchen. Mom was sitting at the table, listening to Rina as she excitedly interpreted a letter for my mother.

Rina comes from Russia. She was a budding gymnast training for the Olympics, when she was surprisingly granted permission to leave Russia. Her parents are refuseniks, and while they're waiting for their exit visas, Rina is living at my house. We get along great. Rina is like the sister I never had.

"Listen," both Rina and I exclaimed together.

"You go first," I said laughingly when I saw Rina's news had excited her so much, she wouldn't be able to control herself.

"No, you speak first," Rina insisted politely.

"Forget it," I said. "My news can wait. But you look as if you are going to burst, you are so excited."

"Well," she began slowly, as if she was trying to keep me in suspense. Her words, then, just came flowing out. "I just received a letter from my parents. They received their exit visas. They're going to be in the States in time for Pesach!"

"Hooray," Sara and I shouted together. We kissed and we hugged and we started dancing around the little kitchen.

"Now," Rina said as we quieted down a little. "What's your exciting news?"

Sara and I sobered up immediately. We exchanged glances, not wanting to frighten anyone. Cautiously, I described to Mom and Rina the suspicious character who had followed us and what had happened outside just a few minutes ago.

Rina walked to the window and carefully lifted the starched white curtain aside.

"Well, there's nobody there now," she said.

We all followed her to the window and peered outside. The street was empty.

"I wonder who he was? And who was the gang that tried to capture him? And why were they all so interested in us?" Sara murmured softly in one breath.

I shivered in response.

2

A SPECIAL MAZAL TOV

A group of us were sitting together in the ninth grade homeroom. We had moved our desks into a circle and were noshing and chatting during this unexpected free period. Today was Monday. Miss Grosswald had assigned a test for Wednesday, which would be the last day of school before Pesach vacation.

The test was on the last two chapters we were assigned to read in the World Geography book. None of us had read the two chapters, and therefore we were very upset at the scheduling of the test.

"Can you believe this teacher?" Sara rhetorically asked nobody but really everybody. "Doesn't she realize it's erev Pesach?"

"Well, maybe she doesn't come from a large family and doesn't understand how much work has to be done with so little time before Pesach," I said, trying to excuse Miss Grosswald. Even as I said the words, I knew this wasn't a legitimate reason.

"I know what I'll do," Sara said, fuming at the unfairness of the assignment. "I'm going to speak to my mother about this!"

Sara's mother is the principal of our school, Rivkah Gross Academy. Sara's always thinking of different ways to use this fact to her advantage. Most of the time, however, it doesn't work. Mrs. Goodman treats Sara the same way she treats all the other high school kids.

"And you know what the response is going to be?" I interrupted Sara.

"Yes, I know," Sara sighed, mimicking her mother, a trait she does rather well. "If you would have just studied a little every night when the teacher assigned the work to you, you wouldn't be cramming at the last minute."

"Well, I'm so glad we have this unexpected free period today," Naomi said.

"Yes," Miriam agreed. "But if Miss Tobias would have been absent on any day besides Monday, we would have been dismissed early."

We all groaned in response. Miriam was right. English, the subject Miss Tobias teaches, is usually the last period of the day. Mondays, however, we have English the next-to-last period because we have Home Economics, a once-a-week course.

"I guess we could be studying," Rina timidly suggested.

I readily agreed with Rina. I knew I would have very little time to study for the World Geography test at home. My mother is the assistant principal of Rivkah Gross Academy. She works a full day. When I come home from school, there are always chores I have to do, especially right before Pesach.

"I've got a great idea," Sara said.

Sara's eyes lit up as she gathered us into a tighter circle.

"Study as best as you can. And then during lunchtime on Wednesday, which is right before the World Geography test is scheduled to begin, I'll tell you what I am planning."

Sara looked extremely satisfied with herself, which made me groan in despair. Whenever Sara has one of these complicated plans of hers, the whole class usually follows her lead. And we all get into lots of trouble.

Oh well, I shrugged to myself. So much could happen before Wednesday. Maybe we wouldn't have to follow the mischief Sara planned.

"I wonder why Miss Tobias is absent," Sara mused. As usual, as soon as Sara makes up her mind, Sara's attention shifts to another topic.

"I heard she comes from Chicago," Naomi stated to no one in particular. "Maybe she went home early to help her family get ready for Pesach."

"That makes a lot of sense," Shira agreed as we all nodded our heads. All, that is, except Sara.

"Nah," Sara said. "I would have known about it by now. Besides which, I'm sure my mother would have found a substitute for the last three days before vacation."

"Yes," I admitted. "It's not like your mother or my mother to let us have a free period. They're much too organized."

"Maybe she got sick the last minute," someone suggested.

Before we could discuss that theory, Layah opened the closed door of the classroom and came running in, breathlessly.

"Hurry up and straighten out the desks. Rabbi Efram and Miss Tobias are coming. Quick!"

As chaos reigned in the classroom, screams were punctuated by moving desks. Papers were hastily thrown away. Nosh was quickly stuffed into our mouths as the door slowly opened.

Rabbi Efram and Miss Tobias walked into the room.

Rabbi Efram is the dean of our school. Looking at his features and his form, one might assume he's not fitted for the position of dean in a girls' high school. His demeanor and attitude, though, command respect. Nobody, absolutely nobody, not even Sara, dares to argue with Rabbi Efram. Yet with all his strong discipline, he's well liked and popular, probably because his judgments and punishments are always fair.

Miss Tobias, our favorite teacher, was smiling from ear to ear. Her eyes were shining with excitement. Taking one look at her, the whole class waited in anticipation for Rabbi Efram to make the announcement. We knew what he was going to say even before the words actually left his mouth.

"Girls," Rabbi Efram began. "Miss Tobias is sorry she's late. There were some personal details she had to take care of. I hope you used this extra time to your benefit. I hear you have a World Geography test scheduled for Wednesday. I know I can depend on your taking this time to study for this test and not wasting it on mischievous plans."

At this last statement, Rabbi Efram glanced at Sara, who flushed guiltily and sank lower into her seat. Even I began to blush, although I hadn't been privy to Sara's plan. Rabbi Efram knows his students well.

"Oh, by the way," Rabbi Efram said as he reached the door and began to exit the classroom. "Miss Tobias deserves a mazal tov. She became a *kallah* last night."

And with a typical Rabbi Efram smile, he left the room.

"Mazal tov!"

We all began singing and dancing. Miss Tobias, flushed and grinning with excitement and happiness, joined in our fun.

After ten minutes of happy and exuberant celebrating, we all crowded around Miss Tobias and listened while she told us about her *chasan*.

"His name is Yaakov Stein. He's learning in Eretz Yisrael and recently returned to America for Pesach."

We greeted this statement with absolute silence. After the hysteria of the last few minutes, the quiet proved to be unsettling and uncomfortable.

Miss Tobias looked at all of us in puzzlement. Finally, her eyes landed on Sara, the only one of the class who would have the nerve to ask Miss Tobias the question that was burning in all our minds.

"Is he going back to Eretz Yisrael after Pesach?" Sara asked, hesitantly.

Miss Tobias nodded. The mood shifted down to actual despair at her response. Miss Tobias again looked questioningly at all of the faces in front of her. Then, seeming to understand, Miss Tobias continued to speak.

"My *chasan* will be returning to Eretz Yisrael for the summer *zeman*," she continued to explain. "After Tishah B'Av, he'll be returning to America, and we're planning to get married in Chicago in August, *b'ezras Hashem*."

Miss Tobias paused to see the effect her words were having on us.

"Of course," she continued, "everybody who can get tickets to Chicago is invited to the wedding."

This statement was greeted by cheers. We all made mental notes to begin saving our money so we could attend Miss Tobias's wedding in Chicago.

Miss Tobias had stopped speaking. We all waited for her to continue and to tell us if she was planning to move to Eretz Yisrael after she was married. This was, of course, the dream each girl had in her mind. Yet we loved Miss Tobias, and she was the best teacher any of us had ever had. Selfishly, we didn't want to see her leave. We all looked to Sara so she could verbalize the thoughts that were in our minds.

"And then..." Sara began.

"And then...what?" Miss Tobias teased.

"Well, after you get married," Sara continued uncomfortably. "Are we intruding if we ask you what your plans are after you get married?"

Sara's stiff politeness caused by her anxiety to know the answer seemed to fill Miss Tobias with a little pity. Her eyes softened as she looked at all of us and answered, "Well, after I get married it will be back to business as usual. You know, tenth grade English tests and tenth grade compositions."

Again, Miss Tobias looked at the circle of questioning eyes.

"That is, if you do all the assignments and pass all the tests required for ninth grade," she concluded. "You will be tenth graders next year, won't you?"

The meaning of her words sunk in. We realized that after Miss Tobias would get married in the summer, she was planning to return as our teacher in the fall. We all breathed a sigh of relief.

"You really scared us there," Sara said accusingly. "Now we can really celebrate!"

The dancing and singing continued another five minutes, until the bell rang to indicate the conclusion of our English period.

3

ARRIVALS AND DEPARTURES

The station wagon seemed empty. Mom had stayed home to finish some last details of Pesach cleaning before the arrival of the Koshevskis. My brothers had volunteered to stay and help. Tatty was driving the car, and humming a happy tune.

Rina, Sara, and I were sitting in the second seat. Rina was a nervous wreck and kept looking at her watch.

"Calm down," I said to Rina as I patted her hand. "Don't worry so much. My father's a good driver. We'll get there in time to meet your parents' plane."

"I know," Rina admitted. "I just can't help it. I've waited for this day for so long. I can't believe it has arrived."

She checked her watch another time.

"In less than two hours I will be seeing my mother and father again," Rina commented. "I just don't believe it!" Surprisingly enough, Sara had hardly said anything during our ride to the airport. She seemed to be very fidgety and kept looking out of the window behind us. I pretended I didn't notice her preoccupation with the cars on the road. I could tell, though, that she was really disturbed.

"I'm so glad we will be spending the next month or so at your house, until my parents can find accommodations," Rina said.

"Oh, don't thank us," I said. "You know my mother. She'd be extremely insulted if you would even think of staying at someone else's house. She takes the mitzvah of *hachnasas orchim* very personally."

"There's the airport," Rina exclaimed as we began noticing the airplanes establishing patterns for landing and taking off.

"Do you think their plane was early? Maybe it landed already! Maybe my parents are standing with their luggage, thinking I have deserted them!"

My father stopped his humming to calm Rina down. "Don't worry," he said. "I called the airport right before we left the house, and everything's proceeding according to schedule. We'll be early enough. You'll probably have some time to walk around and see things before we'll get a chance to meet with your parents."

As Rina finally relaxed, I glanced at Sara. She was sitting in the window seat, next to Rina. How was

I supposed to ask her what the problem was without disturbing Rina? I needn't have worried. Sara found a solution.

"Let's play a game," Sara suggested innocently. "You look out your window and I'll look out mine. You could look in all the lanes where cars are driving. The object of the game is to find a dark-blue little Volkswagen. The first person to find five dark-blue little Volkswagens wins the game."

"I'm too uptight to play," Rina said. "I'm going to close my eyes and try to relax before we reach the parking lot. You two play and have fun."

Rina leaned her head back against the seat and closed her eyes.

I looked at Sara for some signal, but she had already turned around in her seat. In the position she was sitting, she would be able to see the cars in the lane on the left. She could also watch the cars following behind us. I took the same position in my seat at the right of Rina.

"I see one dark-blue Volkswagen," I exclaimed almost immediately.

As I looked out of the window, watching for any more distinctive cars, I noticed that the dark-blue Volkswagen stayed in its position behind our car.

Oh well, I shrugged to myself. It's a free country. Anyone is allowed to use the highways.

"There's the airport!" my father exclaimed.

He slowed the car to turn off the exit ramp toward Newark airport. The dark-blue Volkswagen also exited off the highway.

Well. Anyone can exit off a highway and go to an airport.

My father slowed the car so he could see which terminal the airplane was slated to arrive at.

The dark-blue Volkswagen also slowed down.

Maybe he's also looking for the correct terminal.

"Okay, girls," my father said. "I'll drop you off at the International Arrivals building, and then I will park the car and meet you at the proper gate."

As my father stated these words, he slowed the car to try to find a space on the curb to pull over.

The dark-blue Volkswagen also slowed to a crawl.

The airport was overflowing with business. Cars were dropping off passengers and picking up other passengers and luggage. The scene was one of chaos. The warm smoggy air was punctuated with cries of policemen and the honking of horns. There were squeals of brakes from rushing taxicabs that timed their maneuvers to an inch of their destination. The heavy buses exhausted black plumes of diesel smoke. It was an extremely unpleasant scene, everyone hustling to meet their own schedule. Politeness and courtesy were reserved for a time when airplane schedules were not of importance.

My father smiled. He had been raised in New York and had frequently driven his *rosh yeshivah* around the city streets of New York. He enjoyed the accuracy of precise driving. He quickly found a spot on the curb to let us out, and aggressively parked, letting the car idle.

"Okay, girls?" he questioned with a grin. "I'll see you in about ten minutes."

I opened my door, which was on the curb side, and held it open for Rina and Sara to step out. The dark-blue Volkswagen slowed as if it was about to make a complete stop. A bus then edged in behind it and honked its horn loudly for all to hear. The dark-blue Volkswagen picked up speed and disappeared.

He didn't disappear fast enough.

"Did you see who was following us?" Sara asked, catching her breath.

I swallowed hard and nodded at the same time.

"Was that our friend the Asian in the back seat of the car?" I questioned rhetorically.

Sara nodded and then added, "I really wasn't sure if the car was following us. But for some reason, the car reminded me of the one that picked up our young friend last week. I wonder..."

There she went again, starting a thought and not quite finishing it.

"Yes?" I waited patiently.

"Well," Sara continued. "Do you think it's just coincidence that he's at the airport? Or was he really following us?"

I didn't like Sara's train of thought and tried to deny her air of mystery.

"Come on," I said. "He obviously knows where I live. He also seems to know where we were going. Why should he follow us to the airport?"

Sara shrugged her shoulders.

"Don't ask me," she said. "But you can't deny he's at the airport."

Sara paused.

"Maybe he's just spying on us," she added with a laugh.

We quickly proceeded into the terminal and looked for the waiting room where we should be sitting to await the arrival of Rina's parents. It was a long walk, and the airport was crawling with people.

"Keep together," I insisted. "I don't want to lose any of you."

"Let's find out if my parents' airplane has arrived," Rina suggested.

We walked over to the computer board where arrivals and departures were displayed.

"There it is," Rina exclaimed excitedly. "The plane's on time."

We continued toward our destination. We were a funny group. Rina was anxiously pulling us forward, while Sara was anxiously looking behind us. I was stuck in the middle, trying not to lose either of them.

I knew why Sara was so busy looking behind her. She was checking to see if the guy was still following us. But her activities were causing me great anxiety.

"Are you sure he was the same person?" I whispered to Sara. "Maybe it's just coincidence."

Sara shook her head negatively.

"Well, I don't see him now," I said. "Let's not spoil Rina's reunion with her parents. Here come some people now."

Rina stood anxiously on her tiptoes, looking for her parents.

Suddenly, she saw them. I felt a shiver run down my back as Rina ran, with a cry of happiness, to meet them.

Amid the hugging and kissing, I saw my father coming. Shaking hands with Mr. Koshevski, he greeted him with his little prepared speech.

As Rina hugged her mother, Mr. Koshevski and Tatty began to pick up the luggage and walk toward the exit. Rina put her arm around her mother's waist, and with her other hand she reintroduced us to Mrs. Koshevski. We had met Rina's parents in Russia about six months before, so greeting them now wasn't too awkward.

Tatty and Mr. Koshevski led the procession. Mrs. Koshevski and Rina followed behind them, talking animatedly. Sara and I brought up the rear.

Sara poked me in the ribs. I nearly collapsed. She pointed with her finger behind us. I turned around to look. Standing next to a counter, seemingly oblivious to the crowd and reading a newspaper, stood our friend the Asian.

Sara stifled a giggle.

"Watch this," she said.

Before I could stop her, or even ask her to explain her intentions, Sara walked straight over to the Asian.

"Excuse me," she said. "Have we met before?"

"Sara and Bracha, let's go," I heard my father call.

I grabbed Sara by the hand and hurriedly caught up to my father.

Sara was engulfed in giggles. I was petrified. I couldn't believe that she had the nerve to walk right up and talk to him!

I turned around to look one last time. The guy was folding up his newspaper and walking quickly in the other direction.

"I wonder," I said quietly to Sara when I was finally able to catch my breath. "Are you sure that guy was the same one following us?"

Sara shrugged her shoulders.

"Beats me," she said with a shrug.

4

A TESTY REACTION

"Okay," Sara asked. "Are you all sure about what you are supposed to do?"

We nodded our heads in response.

It was Wednesday, the day for which the World Geography test had been scheduled. We had all hoped for some kind of reprieve, but none was forthcoming. Miss Grosswald was determined to give the test. The administration was equally determined to stand behind her.

We had no choice. Sara's plan was to go into effect. We all sat studiously at our desks. That was part of Sara's instructions. There was to be no misbehavior. We were all supposed to act the part of industrious students. World

Geography was the only thing we were to have on our minds.

Miss Grosswald stormed into the classroom ready to attack. She almost tripped over her own feet in her haste to get to her desk. She looked at us suspiciously, blinking her eyes constantly.

No student moved a muscle. Out of the corner of my eye, I saw every ninth grader sitting at her desk. Everyone's feet were placed squarely on the floor. All hands were folded neatly and quietly on the desks.

"Quiet," Miss Grosswald screeched.

Nobody had made a sound, and so we all swallowed our laughter at Miss Grosswald's typical uneasiness.

"Take out a sharpened pencil or a pen," Miss Grosswald commanded.

Nobody moved a muscle. We had all prepared our pencils and pens before Miss Grosswald had arrived in the classroom.

"I'm going to hand out the test papers to you," Miss Grosswald directed, a little more calmly.

She was surprised at our cooperation, and she still seemed to be just a little suspicious. Sara's plan was really working.

"Answer the questions in your best possible manner," she continued her directions.

Looking at us sitting so politely, her blinking eyes softened a bit in compassion.

"I tried to make this test easy," Miss Grosswald apologized. "I realize it's right before Pesach and studying World Geography isn't your favorite pastime."

I began to feel a little bit guilty. I could tell Sara thought she might be losing a little of her control. She carefully cleared her throat. Our attention was directed back to the task at hand.

Sara's plan was really very simple.

We all had studied for this World Geography test, some of us a little more than others. We weren't trying to get away without taking the test. We just didn't feel the time the test was scheduled was really very fair.

Some of the girls, like Sara, would only have to read the two chapters over one time. They wouldn't have any trouble learning the necessary material. An hour of studying would be enough time for them.

There were other girls, though, who would have to spend five or six hours on reviewing the material. And even then, they would just get a passing grade.

Sara's plan was in defense of these girls. Everybody had been instructed by Sara to study as best as she could, without shirking their Pesach cleaning duties. That we did.

Now it was time to take the test. I found the questions quite easy, but I had studied hard. I knew Sara would find the test a breeze.

"Five minutes left, girls." Miss Grosswald stood up and paced nervously in front of the classroom. What was she expecting us to do to her?

"Okay," she shrilly commanded. "Time's up! Hand in your papers."

Everyone put down their writing instruments and passed up their papers. We all smiled at our friends as we handed our papers in per Miss Grosswald's instructions. Okay. So, big deal. We forgot to put our names on our test papers.

The test papers were now in Miss Grosswald's hands. She put them in a folder without even glancing at them. We all relaxed with a sigh of relief.

Suddenly, the classroom door opened. Rabbi Efram stood at the entrance. Miss Grosswald looked at him and smiled. Rabbi Efram put out his right arm. Miss Grosswald handed him the folder with our test papers. We all watched this unrehearsed play in shock. Rabbi Efram took the folder and left the classroom.

Miss Grosswald fidgeted with the disorder on her desk.

"Class dismissed," she said. "Have a happy Pesach!"

We slowly stood up from behind our desks. Sara flushed guiltily. She hadn't expected Rabbi Efram to get involved with our mischievous prank.

"Oh, well," she shrugged fatalistically. "It's too late to do anything about it now."

"If we get into trouble because of you..." Miriam angrily began to verbally attack Sara.

We all turned around and stared in surprise at Miriam.

"I'm sorry," Miriam apologized. "It's just that I'm frightened."

I was also a little nervous. I knew Rabbi Efram wouldn't allow this deed to go unpunished. But we were all guilty. Even though it had been Sara's plan not to write our names on the test, each and every one of us had cooperated.

"Don't despair." I shrugged, trying to comfort Miriam. If it makes you feel better, we'll all get punished together. What can Rabbi Efram do to *all* of us?"

It didn't take us very long to find out. It was during our last class of the day — English — when Rabbi Efram entered our classroom. He was holding a manila folder in his hand, the folder that held our World Geography tests.

We shifted uncomfortably in our seats. Nobody dared look at anyone else. Rabbi Efram had our full attention. He looked at every one of us in turn. And then he spoke.

"As you are well aware, I am holding your World Geography tests in my hand," Rabbi Efram said, quietly and steadily. "I have saved Miss Grosswald the bother of marking the tests."

Were we going to be saved? Was Rabbi Efram going to trash the tests without even looking at them?

"I marked the tests myself," Rabbi Efram continued.

I groaned inwardly. *Here it comes.*

"Some of the girls in the class did very nicely." He opened up the folder and leafed through the papers. "There were two 100s, about four girls received in the 90s, a few 80s, two 70s..." Rabbi Efram paused. "And ten girls failed."

We all sat frozen in our seats, waiting for Rabbi Efram's judgment.

"I am very proud of the passing grades. And I could tell that the girls who failed the test had put forth some effort and had also studied. I had planned to schedule a retest after Pesach for those who wished."

Rabbi Efram paused again. He looked at each of us in turn. I could see all the girls reacting to Rabbi Efram's news with the same feelings I had. Was I one of the girls who got a 100? Or did I receive a mark in the 90s? Now I'd never know!

"Now that I have the tests in front of me, though," Rabbi Efram continued, "I find I'm not able to be merciful." Rabbi Efram's next sentence was stated with a cold and steady voice, very businesslike.

"Since none of the test papers can be identified, each member of the class will receive the same mark. The scores average a 64. Everyone will receive a 64, which will be decisive in your final report card mark. Have a good yom tov. Class dismissed."

We all sat stunned.

5

AN AFIKOMAN SURPRISE

We left our last class with mixed emotions. On the one hand, we were extremely glad school was over for two weeks. It was great to have a vacation from books, tests, and teachers. But every time we thought of our vacation from tests, we kept hearing Rabbi Efram's words echoing in our ears. Everyone would get a 64 averaged into their final mark in World Geography.

I was glad to see the class wasn't blaming Sara for what had happened. We were sorry we had done what we did. Everyone realized, though, that it was a prank we had all done together. Everyone deserved to get punished.

Sara, however, wasn't accepting the verdict sitting down. I knew Sara well enough to realize she was feeling extremely guilty. When I couldn't find her by our locker, I figured she was seeking a means to get the class punishment lightened. I knew she was probably meeting with Rabbi Efram to take all the punishment upon herself. Such a martyr! I went to meet her outside of Rabbi Efram's office.

I sat on the bench, nervously awaiting Sara's exit. The whole building held an eerie quiet. The janitor was sweeping the hallways, and scraps of papers were dancing in the air.

I jumped when I heard the chairs scraping inside the office, and I heard Sara and Rabbi Efram. I looked to see the results of their talk. Sara was smiling shyly, while Rabbi Efram was wishing her a *gut yom tov*.

"So what happened?" I said, unable to keep quiet. "Don't keep me in suspense!"

"Rabbi Efram's really a good sort of guy," Sara admitted. "He said it didn't matter whose idea it was originally. He said since every single girl had her own personal choice to make, each girl was guilty."

Sara suddenly smiled, and her whole face lit up.

"I apologized for the class, but he said we shouldn't worry."

"Do you think maybe he'll reverse his decision?" I questioned hopefully.

"No, I don't think so," Sara said. "But I got the feeling that now that the prank's been done, we should just go on from here. So why are you so sad? It's erev yom tov!"

Sara and I began walking home. The trees were just beginning to bud, and the air was warm with hints of spring.

"Oh, with the World Geography test and everything else," I said to Sara, "I forgot all about the wonderful news."

"*Nu,*" Sara asked. "So what is it?"

I looked at Sara and shrugged my shoulders.

"I don't know," I said.

"What do you mean you don't know?" Sara asked me, perplexed. "Just two seconds ago you said you had wonderful news. Now you say you don't know what that wonderful news is?"

I nodded my head, and then continued.

"Well, you know how parents are," I continued telling Sara. "Just before I left to school this morning, my father hinted that he had a special surprise for me and a friend. A surprise that might come as an afikoman present."

"Do you have any idea what he's referring to?"

"Nope," I answered. "My parents have been having secret talks. I thought that was because the Koshevskis are visiting and they were busy planning ways for the Koshevskis to feel more comfortable. But now I'm wondering if those talks really have to do with this afikoman surprise."

"Well, keep in touch," Sara said as we reached Marigold Road, where I turned off. "Have a good night."

I continued walking home, my mind wandering and envisioning the surprise. I was so preoccupied, I didn't notice the person ahead of me until I almost bumped into him. He had been standing with his back to me, looking at my house.

"Oh, excuse me," I said, ready to apologize for not watching where I was going.

The person turned around, and when he saw that I recognized his face, he ran off in the opposite direction.

I stood there, hypnotized and frozen in place.

Why was he still watching my house? And as I pondered that thought, my subconscious was making me aware of something else that was quite strange. Why was he so frightened?

I quickly entered the house to tell my mother what had happened outside. The house was whirling with erev Pesach preparations.

"Are you the new janitor?" my brother Yudie teased. "Really, though, it's your job to lock up all the *chametzdik* closets. Get to it!"

I frowned at Yudie, wanting to tell him about the Asian. I was afraid he would laugh at me.

"And don't forget to clean out your school bag and your purse before Pesach," Yudie added. "Who knows what kind of chametz you're carrying around."

I started up the stairs, waiting for Yudie's parting statement, knowing there was still more that he had to tease me about.

"And hurry up into the kitchen and start peeling potatoes and apples," he concluded. "We *all* love potato kugel and apple kugel."

I felt an urge to argue with him, but the truth of the matter is, he was right. As this was my first year in high school, Mom had been more lenient with me than with the boys. I had helped as much as possible, but Mom hadn't really demanded from me the same amount of work she'd demanded from my brothers.

I quickly did my assigned jobs and ran to help Mom in the kitchen.

The kitchen was bubbling with activity. Mrs. Koshevski was busy making borscht. Mom was taking the third chocolate brownie cake out of the oven. Rina had been excused from school today because of the arrival of her parents, and was whipping up ice cream. I quickly sat down at the table, potato peeler in hand. I began my job.

The kitchen smells were delicious.

"I can't wait for the Seder," I said to no one in particular.

"I can," Mom answered. "I'm glad we still have a few more days. Although with Shabbos in between, everything seems more overwhelming. Whatever can be done before Shabbos will make erev Pesach somewhat calmer. Then we'll still have the charoses to make and the maror to check. That will be the boys' job on Sunday."

I knew I didn't have any reason to worry. The evening passed by quickly, and I went to sleep with the smell of potato kugel permeating the air.

I awakened the next morning to even more delicious smells. As I lay in bed, the delicious sweet-and-spicy aroma of gefilte fish drifted up to my bedroom.

I quickly said *Modeh Ani*, jumped out of bed, washed *negel vasser* and got dressed.

Skipping lightly down the stairs, I saw that only Mom was in the kitchen. She was sitting at the table, eating a piece of Pesach cake and drinking a cup of coffee.

"I'll be right with you to help," I said. "As soon as I finish davening."

"Don't hurry," Mom said. "Everything's under control. We probably cooked enough food last night that I won't have to cook anything for the second days of yom tov."

Mom and I smiled at each other. This special feeling of camaraderie was new for us. But it really warmed me up inside.

Throughout the preparations, I kept watching Rina and her parents, wondering what feelings they were having. Last Pesach, they had been in Russia. How would this Pesach compare?

We were all sitting around the Seder table. We were up to *Shulchan Orech* and were just finishing the last bits of pareve ice cream. I looked at my father with awe.

Tatty had so much patience. I remembered how he would explain the Seder to us when we were children. He would ask us all questions and listen with great patience to our answers and *divrei Torah*.

This Pesach was unusual. This was the first Pesach Rina and her parents were celebrating in freedom. Rina's father listened and followed everything Tatty did. But once it came to the meal, I saw he finally was willing to relax.

During the meal, Rina's father described their Pesach last year. He told us that the previous year they had all sat around the Pesach table in fear of being discovered, and they had prayed *l'shanah haba'ah bnei chorin*, next year to be free.

"This year," Mr. Koshevski said, "when those words left my lips, I knew I was free of the Russian yoke. I was free to daven and serve Hashem as I always wanted to. Now that the part of being free has come true, I know the next line will also come true. *L'shanah haba'ah b'Yerushalayim*, next year in Jerusalem."

We all answered, "Amen. Mashiach should come right now."

"But," my father said, "while we're waiting for Mashiach, I think it's time for me to search for the afikoman."

My brothers and I exchanged glances. They had stolen the afikoman from my father. But when they weren't looking, or so I thought, I had stolen the afikoman from them.

My father went through his act of searching for the afikoman.

"Okay, Yudie," my father asked my oldest brother. "Where is it?"

Yudie looked around his seat.

"Sorry, Tatty," he said. "I thought I had it, but I can't seem to find it."

Tatty heaved a pretend sigh.

"Now what am I going to do?" Tatty pretended to despair. "Okay, Sruly, where is it?"

Sruly also looked around his seat. I began to suspect everyone was part of some plan involving the afikoman and me.

"Sorry, Tatty," Sruly said. "I can't seem to find it either." Tatty looked at me. So did everyone else sitting at the table.

"Well, what makes you think I know where the afikoman is?" I began to protest.

My parents exchanged glances.

"Well," Tatty said, stalling. "I guess you won't get this very special surprise for afikoman."

With these words, Tatty took out a long white envelope from his pocket.

I quickly brought the afikoman, but before I gave it to my father, I still wanted to know what was in the envelope as my reward.

Tatty held the envelope teasingly away from my grasp. "Well, in this envelope is a special treat. It's something that you are to share with Sara."

First Tatty opened the envelope, ever so slowly. He then took out a sheet of paper, opened it up, and began to recite the poem written on it.

"An invitation came one week
About a trip where you should go
A bar mitzvah celebration
A week in San Francisco
The boys can't leave yeshivah
Mom has too much to do
Tatty has to work in the city
So, Bracha and Sara, the air tickets are for you."

I sat stunned.

"Hurray," everyone shouted.

"You mean you didn't suspect a thing?" Rina asked.

I still couldn't believe what I had just heard.

"You mean Mom and you aren't going to San Francisco?" I finally managed to gasp out.

"Nope," Tatty said, grinning. "We never planned on going. This was the surprise afikoman present we had been planning all along. Sara's getting a companion ticket. Now, let's have the afikoman and continue with the Seder."

6

OFF AT LAST

I can't believe I'm here," Sara said for about the hundredth time. "Can you?"

"The time has flown by so quickly," I answered. "It seems like just yesterday I was sitting at the Seder table, waiting for my father to find the afikoman."

"I couldn't believe it," Sara remarked. "It hadn't even dawned upon *my* devious mind that your parents and my parents were planning this surprise."

"I guess we're just two very lucky people." I sighed. "I wonder what's taking this plane so long? Weren't we supposed to take off at six thirty?"

"I don't know," Sara answered as she looked out of

the window. "It's six thirty now, and the cargo door is still open."

"Good evening, passengers, this is your captain speaking," we heard the announcement over the microphone. "I'm sorry that we're having a short delay. There are some technical details being solved in the cargo hold. As soon as I know more information, I will be glad to inform you. In the meantime, please sit back and enjoy yourselves."

"He's funny," Sara commented. "How am I supposed to enjoy myself if I'm so anxious to be in San Francisco already?"

Sara and I peered out the airplane window. We were seasoned travelers already, having gone to Russia earlier in the year. But we were still very anxious and excited about this trip.

"Do you know?" Sara questioned. "We've been so excited about this trip, you haven't told me very much about your cousins in California. I'm not even sure I remember their name."

"Well, their last name is also Friedman. They're not my first cousins. I think they're my second cousins. We share the same Zeidy, you know, my Zeidy that lives in Eretz Yisrael, my father's father's father."

"How did they get to San Francisco?" Sara asked. "And why do they stay out there, so far away from Yiddishkeit?"

I sat back and thought a little about what my father had explained to me.

"When my father's Zeidy first came to America from Poland, it was in the early 1900s," I said. "There were a few yeshivos around, and all my father's Zeidy's children went to the yeshivos. But after they graduated high school, everyone had to find a job so they could help support the family.

"My Zeidy, being the oldest, helped his father in the jewelry business. His father was a watchmaker, and my grandfather began selling precious gems over the counter. My father works with my grandfather, but he specializes in buying and selling antique jewelry. As a matter of fact, that's what my father was doing in Chinatown before Pesach. He was arranging the purchase of some rare gems from the Orient. All my uncles are partners in the jewelry business, each specializing in different aspects of the jewelry trade.

"My Zeidy's brothers and sisters, however, all moved to different parts of the world. They went into their spouses' family businesses. This specific son was sent overseas to France during the Second World War. There he met a French girl whose family worked for a winemaker. For a while, my great-uncle lived in France and learned the business. He said, though, he missed the freedom and advantages that American Jews have. He moved the family back to America.

"They lived for a while in New York, working for my Zeidy. But my great-aunt was unhappy with the climate, and my great-uncle felt his heart wasn't into the business. He really loved making wine, and so he moved out to California."

I hesitated now, because this was the part of the story I myself was finding hard to understand. Tatty had tried to explain to me the emotions of the times, in the early 1950s. I still couldn't understand how anyone would want to leave the center of Yiddishkeit in the East, just because of the lure of money or career happiness in the Golden Gate of the West. I remembered arguing with Tatty about how wrong Great-Uncle Murray had been. His family had not remained *frum*.

"We're sorry for the further delay," the captain interrupted over the microphone. "You're not going to believe what's happening down there in the cargo hold. They've been trying to tie down a small compact car for transport to San Francisco. The report is they've almost completed this task, and we should be on our way in a few minutes."

"A car," Sara repeated. "I don't believe it! Can the cargo hold fit such a large object as a car?"

"Well, they said it was a compact," I observed.

"Some compact," Sara joked. "Oh, well. Continue."

"So my great-uncle moved to the land of golden opportunities, California. He bought a small vineyard out in Sonoma County, an area that's very respected for wine growing. After a while, his vineyard became well known. The grapes he produced were very popular. My great-uncle then decided he was going to learn more about the actual wine-making process. He became apprenticed to a famous nonkosher wine maker, and learned the proper process. For many years, he learned the different methods and began experimenting with his own wine at home.

"His son Barry continued with the family business, taking care of the vineyard and experimenting on his own.

When he decided to go to college to learn the chemistry involved in wine making, his father encouraged him. Needless to say, at this point, nobody in the family was still *frum*. It was impossible to uphold the strict observance Great-Uncle Murray had been taught in Zeidy's home. Nobody else in Sonoma valley was even Jewish, never mind *frum*. So it wasn't surprising that Barry was raised completely nonobservant.

"When Barry married, it was lucky he married a Jewish girl. He had happened to meet her brother at college. Since they were one of the few Jewish people in the college, they associated together. And now comes the most interesting part of the story."

"Hi, again. This is the captain." My story was interrupted another time. "You may walk around the airplane. The crew down in the hold has decided they cannot properly anchor the compact car. They have decided to remove the car and shift the rest of the cargo to rebalance the cargo hold. All beverages and snacks are compliments of the airline. Again, sorry for the delay."

"I think if I retell what has happened on this airplane to any one of our friends," Sara commented, "they would never believe us."

"For sure," I agreed. "Anyhow, let me continue.

"Barry had been working for a couple of years for the same wine company as Murray did. He, however, was so successful, he was approached by a kosher wine company to direct their operations. As they explained the strict laws of kashrus necessary to produce a kosher wine to Barry, he began to get more involved with Yiddishkeit itself. Soon he became *shomer Shabbos* and *shomer Torah u'mitzvos*. He couldn't continue to live in Sonoma County, where there are still very few Jews, while he was raising a family. So he moved to the San Francisco area."

"How *frum* are they now?" Sara queried.

"They have three children," I answered. "The oldest daughter, Shoshi, is seventeen. She goes to Bais Yaakov of Denver. The son, Menachem, is turning bar mitzvah now, and he's in the seventh grade in the day school in San Francisco. The little girl, Honey, is seven, and she's in the first grade in the day school. I guess you could say they're as *frum* as we are. But knowing where the family has come from, and living amongst so many Jews who are very assimilated, they're probably stronger in Yiddishkeit than most yeshivah kids."

Sara thought my last statement over for a minute and then questioned me further.

"What makes you think that they're more *frum* than we are?"

"No, I didn't say that they're more *frum*," I insisted. "I said they're probably *stronger*. I mean, take a look at Rina. Because she was denied the luxury of living a *frum* life in Russia, she treasures each mitzvah that comes her way. My cousins value each mitzvah and try to do them very carefully. We, unfortunately, are much more lax. We take kashrus for granted to such a degree that we don't even value our *chalav Yisrael* milk and glatt kosher meat. My mother said that until a few years ago they had to ship their meat and cheeses from Los Angeles because there wasn't even a reliable kosher food store. Luckily

Barry's sister-in-law married a *frum* guy from New York who opened up a reliable grocery shop and butcher store."

Sara nodded her head as she agreed with me.

"Come," she said. "Let's take a walk around the cabin and get some soda to drink."

My arms and legs were getting cramped, and so I readily agreed with her. We got up to stretch and began walking down the aisle, Sara leading the way. After only a few steps, she stopped and turned around quickly. Immediately we bumped into each other.

"Hey, what's the matter?" I questioned Sara in surprise.

"Walk in the other direction," Sara commanded.

I followed her instructions, knowing never to question Sara about her strange behavior. After we walked about ten steps, Sara began to calm down.

"Turn around very slowly," she said. "Tell me if you recognize anyone you know."

I slowly followed her instructions. I looked at all the faces of the people who were milling about. Some people were acting quite festive while others were undeniably disturbed with the unexpected delay.

"Nope," I answered. "I don't see anyone I know."

"Can you see the people who are sitting in the row behind us?" Sara asked.

"Nope," I answered and proceeded to nonchalantly walk back past our seat. I almost froze with shock.

Sitting right behind us and probably listening to our whole conversation was a figure we had come to recognize. I felt I knew the guy already. It was the person who had been following us ever since our ride on the bus from the shopping center. It was the thin and slight Asian.

Yet although I was frightened to see his face so near to us, I felt the look in his eyes beginning to haunt me. The youth was sitting in the middle seat, kind of strapped in between two large Asian men. The boy looked at me and seemed to recognize me. But those haunted black eyes seemed to be telling me a different story. I got the feeling he was frightened, maybe even terrified.

"Will everyone please be seated?" I heard the captain's voice from a distance. "Please fasten your seat belts, and check that your seats are in the upright position. We have finally been cleared for liftoff."

Walking like a robot, I mechanically did as the captain ordered. I quietly awaited the air trip to San Francisco.

"I wonder if it's just coincidence that he's on the same airplane as us," Sara said. "Or if he's really following us."

"I'll tell you the truth," I whispered my theory. "I'm not too sure what's happening here. Did you see those two thugs?"

"Yeah," Sara nodded. "They look like gangsters. Do you think they're all partners?"

"I don't know," I answered. "But I don't think that kid chose his companions."

"And to tell the truth," Sara continued her musings, "he doesn't seem too overjoyed to be on this airplane flight." I could only shrug my shoulders in response.

7

EAST COAST, WEST COAST

The flight went by really fast. I guess because we had started an hour later than we expected, and adding the effect of our shadowy follower sitting behind us, we found we didn't want to talk very much.

Sara and I both read the new novels we had brought along. Before we expected it, it was time to land.

"What time is it?" Sara yawned.

"Believe it or not, it's one thirty in the morning," I answered, rubbing my eyes from tiredness. "That's Eastern Standard time, of course."

"What's the time difference between the East Coast and the West Coast?" Sara began calculating. "Let's see, there's a three-hour time difference. That means it's ten thirty San Francisco time."

The airplane circled for a few minutes and then cruised to a safe and smooth landing.

We gathered our hand luggage from beneath our seats. Sara stood on my seat and opened up the over-head storage compartment to get out our spring jackets. When we had left Pineville, it had been warm and very springlike. During the daytime, jackets weren't even necessary. But everyone insisted that although the days in San Francisco were pleasant, the nights would be quite cool. So we had followed everyone's advice and had taken our Shabbos spring jackets with us.

"How are you going to recognize your cousins?" Sara asked as we waited for the slow-moving line of passengers to disembark.

"Beats me," I answered, shrugging. "I guess we'll just have to look lost, and I'm sure someone will come save us."

As the line continued to move slowly toward the exit, Sara and I wordlessly managed to place a few passengers in between the Asians and ourselves.

Soon we found ourselves approaching the cabin doors and exiting into the passageway toward the waiting room. I found myself searching the waiting crowd, looking for a familiar face.

"Bracha and Sara, over here," I heard someone cry out.

I followed the sound of the voice, and there was some-one who most definitely was my cousin Shoshi, beckoning for us to go in her direction.

Amid the hellos and hugs and kisses, I finally ventured to ask my question.

"How did you know it was us?" I wanted to know.

"Well," Shoshi answered, "your mother gave very specific descriptions. Anyhow, all I had to look for was two Bais Yaakov girls. Look around and tell me if you can find anyone else fitting that description."

I looked at the crowd that was leaving the airplane and also at the group of people meeting them. Shoshi was right. We *did* look different. We were the only two teenagers wearing skirts and long-sleeved blouses. Even our hairstyles were more conservative than everyone else's.

"I never thought to look for that," I said to Shoshi and saw that Sara was nodding her agreement. "Back in Pineville *everyone* dresses *tzniusdik*. We blend in with the crowd. Whenever we have interschool functions, it's also with Bais Yaakov—type schools."

"Look at you," Sara added. "You also dress like a Bais Yaakov girl."

She then stuffed her hand over her mouth.

"Oh, I'm sorry," she said. "I didn't mean to offend you."

"Don't worry." Shoshi smiled. "You didn't insult me. I dress like a Bais Yaakov girl because I *am* a Bais Yaakov girl. But there are very few of our type in San Francisco."

We looked at her inquiringly.

"You'll see what I mean soon," she said. "In the meantime, let's go get your baggage." And she proceeded to lead us toward the baggage area. "Oh, by the way," Shoshi added. "If for some reason I wouldn't have known who you were, your mother sent this to us."

And Shoshi handed us a recent snapshot of Sara and me dancing at a *simchas yom tov* during Chol HaMoed Pesach.

I could tell we were going to have a lot of fun during this week. Shoshi seemed to be the type of girl who would help us get the most out of this San Francisco vacation.

As we waited for the luggage to be expelled onto the revolving carousel, Shoshi discussed the itinerary for our visit.

"It's now Wednesday night," she said. "We'll give you an opportunity to sleep late tomorrow morning, and then we'll do a quick trip into San Francisco proper. First we'll visit Fisherman's Wharf, and then we'll take a cruise around San Francisco Bay. That way, you'll have a chance to see a little of the city.

"By the way," she continued, "the actual bar mitzvah Shabbos celebration isn't going to be in San Francisco. My father felt that since the homes around the shul aren't spacious enough to accommodate the out-of-town guests and his business associates, we rented a hotel in one of the most beautiful areas south of San Francisco. We'll go there early Friday morning so I can take you on a tour of Seventeen Mile Drive. It's a highway that is truly magnificent.

"On Shabbos is my brother Menachem's bar mitzvah. This is going to be a bar mitzvah celebration that San Francisco hasn't seen for a very long time, or even at all. My grandfather, father, and Menachem are doing all the davening and conducting everything. And, by the way, my mother and my aunts did most of the cooking for the bar mitzvah.

"You see, we have this problem with kashrus. The only kosher caterer who is reliable is my uncle. My mother didn't want to overburden him, and so the whole family pitched in to do the cooking. Being that the bar mitzvah is right after Pesach, it really caused a lot of frenzied work. But all the cooking is actually finished."

Just then, I noticed my luggage arriving. We walked over to the carousel and lifted the suitcase off. Almost immediately after, Sara's luggage followed. Shoshi continued speaking.

"Sunday," she said, "we will be going up to my family's vineyard in Sonoma valley. There we will watch the whole process of wine making from start to finish. It's really very interesting. I'm sure my father plans to give you some bottles of wine to take home.

"Sunday night we'll sleep in Sonoma County, and then on Monday, we'll do some touring in that area of California.

"On Tuesday we'll spend some time in San Francisco, touring Alcatraz. You know that used to be a prison. And then we'll do some shopping in Chinatown."

"I can't believe you'll have time to take us touring like this," I questioned Shoshi. "Are we the only out-of-town guests?"

"No," Shoshi answered. "But you certainly have come the farthest. You're the only guests coming from the East Coast. Besides, my cousins and aunts are all assigned someone or some family to take touring. I chose to be in charge of you two."

"Why?" Sara asked. "Although, I could see that you have mapped out a lot of fun times."

"Well, mainly because," Shoshi answered, "I feel most comfortable with you. Some of the guests aren't as *frum* as we are. I'm always having to explain why I dress the way I do and speak the way I do. I know the children of my parents' friends from Sonoma, and they might be the same age as I am. But, boy, are they different. I'm not even familiar with the things that excite them. It's a pleasure to just be able to be myself. I sometimes feel very tired when I pretend to be interested in things I have no idea about."

Sara stifled a giggle.

"That must be funny," she said. "Imagine it the other way around. You could be talking about Professor Green and the Simcha Machine. They would ask you what new kind of music that is and where can you see that rock group perform?"

We all began to laugh and started schlepping the suitcases to where Shoshi had parked the car.

"It's not very far," she said. "Would you rather I pull the car up in front?"

"Nah," we answered bravely and continued carrying the suitcases, pushing and pulling.

"Almost there," Shoshi said, and then walked ahead.

As she did so, we heard some screams and yells behind us. We began to turn around to see what the fuss was about, when a cold and clammy hand thrust itself in front of my face. Sara was receiving the same treatment, as the Asian youth who had followed us in Pineville pushed his way through the exiting crowd of people to be swallowed up behind the darkened cars in the parking lot.

Almost immediately, the two thugs who had been sitting next to him on the airplane started shoving their way through. Good friends usually think alike, and so without any verbal agreement, Sara and I clumsily set our suitcases at the proper angle to trip the two followers.

As they sprawled on the floor trying to gain their balance and their victim, they conversed angrily in Chinese.

"Sorry," I muttered, not very wholeheartedly.

At the sound of my voice, the two thugs looked at Sara and me quite sternly. I felt uncomfortable as they seemed to memorize my face. We quickly grabbed our assorted parcels and headed toward the car.

When we reached it, I couldn't help but turn around to see if the thugs had recaptured the Asian youth.

Sara gave a sigh of relief.

"I think he escaped," she said.

Shoshi took out the key and opened up the trunk. We all piled into the car.

Shoshi sat in the front seat, put the key into the ignition and turned on the lights, but didn't begin moving the car. Then it dawned on me.

"Do you know what we just did?" I asked Sara rhetorically, because I wasn't going to give her an opportunity to answer. "We let that guy escape!"

Sara began to giggle.

"Yeah," she said, punctuating the sentence with another laugh. "We let him escape so he can follow us some more."

Soon all three of us began to laugh.

"We're nuts!" Sara said.

"That's for sure," I agreed, as we filled Shoshi in on all the details of our adventures back in Pineville.

"You know," she said. "I don't want to scare you. But you girls are really very innocent of what's happening in this world."

Sara and I exchanged glances in the dark.

"You're just looking at these incidents as a great adventure," Shoshi warned us. "But you might have walked right into a gang war."

"A what?" Sara asked, flabbergasted.

"A gang war," Shoshi repeated. "If those toughs whom you tripped are part of a gang involved in a war, you might have invited disaster."

I knew Shoshi was talking dramatically, but her words still frightened me. I couldn't forget how carefully the two toughs had memorized my features. What if they decided to take their revenge on us?

I frowned as I envisioned my nice, peaceful bar mitzvah celebration and family reunion marred by a frightening mystery. Sara, however, was sitting at attention, leaning forward in anticipation of the forthcoming excitement.

"Lighten up," Shoshi added as she saw my downcast face. "Our plans aren't changed. We'll *still* have a ball."

We sat silently in the dark car, as Shoshi reversed and began driving out of the parking lot. I had mixed emotions. I was a bit frightened to realize that our playful dramatization of someone following us was a reality. And I certainly didn't want to be stuck in the middle of a gang war. At the same time, I was glad we had interfered and the youth was able to escape. However, now that we had involved Shoshi,

I began to feel more secure. I turned to take a look at how Sara was reacting to Shoshi's information.

I needn't have worried. Even in the dark, I could see Sara's eyes sparkling.

"Okay, Sara," I said. "I see you can't hold it in. Out with it."

"Well," Sara protested innocently. "I just figured that when we take that boat trip to Alcatraz, we'll make sure our friend is following. Ergo, his shadowers, the Chinese toughs, will also be following. Then..."

She paused dramatically.

"Then we'll capture the gang, lock them up inside one of the prison cells, and let the young kid escape. And then..." Sara paused again.

"And then," she added grimly, "maybe we can force out of him why he was following us in Pineville."

Sara, Shoshi, and I nodded together in agreement. We seemed to be agreeing to a silent pact.

8

READY, SET, TOUR

I awakened the next morning, not quite sure where I was. The sun was streaming through the bedroom window. I noticed Sara beginning to stretch in her bed, next to mine.

"What time is it?" she yawned, without even opening her eyes.

I peered at my watch through squinting eyes and bolted upright in the bed.

"Yikes," I gasped. "I can't believe it! It's two o'clock in the afternoon."

Sara just turned over on her side in her bed and yawned again.

"That's New Jersey time," she said. "It's really eleven o'clock California time."

I didn't even remember what time we had gone to sleep. We had arrived at my cousins' house somewhere around four o'clock in the morning, New Jersey time. I tried to remember what my cousin Judy, Barry's wife, looked like. It was all a big blur.

There was a knock on the door, and Shoshi stuck her head in.

"Good morning, girls," she said. "It's about time you sleeping beauties decided to emerge from your castles. Hurry up and get dressed and daven so we still have time to do some touring before supper."

We quickly followed Shoshi's advice and followed the sounds into the kitchen area, clutching our siddurim in our hands.

"You can daven in the living room," Shoshi directed. "And then come into the kitchen, and we'll reintroduce you."

We did as we were told and then shamefacedly ventured into the kitchen.

"We're sorry we slept so late," I began.

"Don't apologize," Judy softly interrupted. "It takes a while to get used to the change in time. Sit down and eat some brunch, and I'll introduce you to people as they arrive. Sometimes, I think this house is the Greyhound Bus Depot, it's so busy."

As Judy spoke, I tried to notice if there were any differences between her and my mother. I couldn't find any. She looked, acted, dressed, and talked just like any *frum* mother. Her hair was completely covered with a *tichel*. She was dressed in a simple blouse and skirt. She wore stockings on her feet. I felt like I was just at home.

As the guests and family started roaming in, though, I started to see differences.

First Naomi, Judy's sister, arrived. She dressed the same as Judy.

Then Menachem, the bar mitzvah boy, came running into the kitchen. He waved hello to us, grabbed a fruit off the table, said a loud berachah, and ran right back outside to his baseball game. He reminded me of my brother Sruly just three years ago. Menachem's shirt-tail was untucked and his tzitzis were also flying. There were no differences there.

When Ruthy came in, though, I began to see the changes in the generations. Ruthy was Murray's wife, Shoshi's grandmother. She was the one who had been born in France, the one who had come to Golden California. She and Murray were the ones who had originally assimilated. I could see that although she was definitely *frum*, the California lack of Yiddishkeit had certainly left its mark on her.

It wasn't only the way Ruthy dressed. These were just outer signs of the permanent changes inside of her. I didn't want to be judgmental. I could see, though, when Ruthy walked into the room, the topics of conversation immediately shifted.

At first Shoshi, Judy, and Naomi were describing the day school and the San Francisco community to us. They tried to explain to us how extremely delicate the Yiddishkeit was.

"It's sooo hard," Shoshi was saying. "When I come home from the Bais Yaakov in Denver, all my friends who graduated with me from the day school have such different priorities. It's like they're in a different world. Go to the movies, go to the beach..."

She immediately silenced herself, though, when her grandmother walked in. Judy quickly changed the subject.

"How did you enjoy your walk, Mother?" she asked Ruthy with great respect. "Did you meet any of your friends?"

"Oh, yes," Ruthy answered, still with a faint trace of a French accent. "I met Olga and Jenny. I'll be going over to Olga's house after lunch. They'll be counting me in their weekly mah jong group, since Terry is out of town this week."

As we proceeded with some small talk, and I gave everyone detailed regards from my family, the telephone rang and Shoshi went to answer it. Immediately, she returned and whispered something to her mother, who quickly went to take the call. When Judy returned, she had a message for us.

"That was Detective Solomon on the telephone," she said. "He and another detective will be here shortly to interview you about your Asian friend. Finish breakfast and bentsh. He should be here in about fifteen minutes."

I noticed that Judy wasn't discreet in mentioning the detectives and the upcoming interview. Shoshi noticed my surprise.

"Let me explain," she said. "Detective Solomon has recently become involved in the security at our wine factory.

There have been some threats and mischief-making stunts taking place at the winery. There were hints that some gangs from Chinatown might be involved. When you went to sleep last night, I told my parents about what had happened at the airport and back in Pineville. Detective Solomon doesn't think there is any connection, but he would like to question you anyhow."

Shoshi paused and then smiled.

"Detective Solomon has been coming to our house so frequently, I think he wants to become a member of the family."

"Either that," Naomi said, "or he just loves your mother's cooking. Did you notice how he always manages to come around at meal time?"

Everyone in the kitchen laughed. I didn't understand why, until fifteen minutes later when Detective Solomon walked into the room.

He certainly didn't look like a detective. Detective Solomon was short, about five foot three. He was also round, all the way around. He looked more like a jolly clown than a serious detective. He introduced himself and his partner, Detective Wong, to Sara and me. He then took a creased, black silk yarmulke out of his pocket. He carefully made a berachah on the piece of cake and the cup of coffee that appeared in front of his seat. Honey, my seven-year-old cousin, nodded her approval.

"See, Detective Solomon," she said. "Now you look Jewish, you act Jewish, and you even talk Jewish."

Everyone laughed. Shoshi led us into the living room.

She explained to us about Detective Solomon while he was finishing off his snack.

"When Detective Solomon started coming around, Honey decided that his name sounded Jewish. She, of course, asked him if he was Jewish, and when he answered in the affirmative, Honey decided she was going to teach him to be *frum.*

"I guess," she added, "if an adult would have tried it, Detective Solomon would probably have been offended. But since it's an innocent little seven-year-old trying, he patiently tolerates it. Besides, who knows? Maybe Honey's perseverance will pay off."

"Either that," Sara answered, "or like your Aunt Naomi said, it more likely has to do with your mother's cooking."

We all laughed again, but stopped quickly as Detectives Solomon and Wong entered the living room and sat down on the couch. Gone were the jokes and the teasing. The two were extremely businesslike and direct in their questioning.

Sara and I told them all we knew. We tried to give a description of all the Asians, but other than their approximate ages, we found ourselves quite at a loss.

"I'm sorry," I apologized. "But a lot of Asian people look the same to us."

"Even I?" Detective Wong questioned.

"No," Sara answered impulsively. "You're built differently, with a little more muscle. And your face is rounder. So are your eyes," she added as an afterthought. Detective Wong smiled.

"That's because I'm not Chinese," he answered. "I am of Hawaiian descent."

"Well." Detective Solomon closed his notebook with a flourish as he completed writing his notes. "Don't worry about a thing. We will be keeping an eye on you. Just go about your business as usual. If you see any of those people following you again, give us a call. We might be lucky enough to find out what this thing is all about."

After the two detectives left, Shoshi hustled us into the car, and we drove through the streets of San Francisco. Everything was very hilly, and the scenery was really beautiful.

"Do people actually live in these houses?" Sara questioned Shoshi as she drove slowly down an extremely steep hill.

"You bet," Shoshi answered. "As a matter of fact, some of these homes are considered to be situated in a really elite neighborhood, very fancy."

"Do any *frum* Jews live around these neighborhoods?" I continued questioning.

"Not that I know of," Shoshi answered. "Why?"

"I was just wondering about the hard walk someone would have coming home from shul, up a steep hill, in any of these neighborhoods."

We all groaned as we imagined it.

"It's a shame it doesn't snow here," Sara added. "Can you imagine the sled rides we could have?"

We laughed together until Shoshi said, "If you want to see a steep hill, just hold on."

She then proceeded to drive us toward a very colorful and flowery block.

"Don't look down," Shoshi warned, and of course we did look down. What we saw was unbelievable.

"This is Lombard Street. It's the most crooked street in the world."

We oohed and aahed appropriately. The road going down Lombard Street wasn't a straight path from top to bottom, but rather it curved in a series of S-curves.

"I can understand why the street was made this way," I commented. "But how do they get a moving van down this hill?"

Shoshi wouldn't take her eyes off of this road for a split second.

"Beats me," she said. "But I'm having enough trouble driving this car."

When we reached the bottom of Lombard Street, Sara finally commented on the last ten minutes.

"I'm sure glad you have good brakes," she said.

"So am I," Shoshi agreed with relief.

Our next stop was Fisherman's Wharf. Before we took our promised scenic boat ride around San Francisco Bay, Shoshi took us on a tour of the shops in the area. We then walked around the different shops that displayed their tourist wares on the docks. Practically every second store housed some sort of food establishment. And yet there was hardly anything kosher.

"Maybe your uncle should open up a fast food place here in Fisherman's Wharf," Sara commented to Shoshi.

"Look around you," Shoshi answered. "How much business do you think he'd get? I haven't seen one yarmulke amongst all these hundreds of people."

"I guess you're right." Sara nodded her agreement. "But I'm hungry!"

"Stop complaining," I advised Sara with a laugh. "Let's take a look in this shop. It sells only chocolate. Maybe we could find a candy bar that has a proper *hash-gachah* on it."

We walked into the dimly lit store and searched up and down the aisles.

"Hey, here's something with rabbinical supervision." Sara pointed to a large bar of chocolate.

"It's really cute," Shoshi said.

The chocolate bar was molded in the shape of a birthday card. Stamped on top were the words "Happy Birthday."

"No good," I commented as I read the ingredients. "It's milchig, but it's not *chalav Yisrael.*"

"Oh, well." Sara shrugged. "It's cute anyway."

"Oh, my goodness," Shoshi exclaimed, a little further up the aisle. "Look at this big chocolate teddy bear!"

"Not kosher, of course," Sara commented. "The smells here in this shop are overwhelming. My stomach is beginning to growl."

And then I spied the ultimate chocolate surprise.

"Take a look at this," I called to Sara. "You must take a picture of this and send it home to your sister Miriam. Too bad *this* isn't kosher."

Standing on a shelf, wrapped in its own paper wrapper and enclosed in a rectangular box, was the solution for every five-year-old. It was a chocolate Band-Aid, for the cuts and scrapes that don't bleed.

We all left the store, laughing contentedly, and proceeded toward the dock.

"San Francisco Bay, here we come."

9

THE CRIME IS COMMITTED

After the boat ride, we returned to Shoshi's house, with glowing cheeks and spirits to match. We had had a magnificent afternoon, and we were ravenous.

"I think we drank about five gallons of soda each," Sara commented.

"That's only because you were so hungry," I teased her. "We had to fill your stomach with *something*."

When we pulled up to the house and parked the car, we were surprised to see how hard it was to find a parking space on the block.

"The other guests are beginning to arrive," Shoshi said. "Come on inside, and I'll introduce you to everyone."

As we walked up the steps of the house, we talked and joked about the scenes we just toured. Sara was aiming her camera at us, taking candid pictures of all our unusual poses. As we reached the door, my back was to it, as Shoshi and I both posed as clowning figures.

Suddenly, the door opened up behind us. I tried to regain my balance, only to be shoved aside by a fleeing figure. I stood up and tried to dust off my skirt. As Shoshi and I turned around, the entrance was again blocked, this time by a young woman.

"Hi, Aunt Ahuvah," Shoshi greeted the young lady as she kissed her cheek.

Aunt Ahuvah smiled slightly as she looked off, worriedly, at the fleeing figure.

I was finding it hard to maintain my composure as I turned around toward Sara. Sara's eyes were also following the running figure.

She turned around to face me and was about to speak, when she saw Shoshi's Aunt Ahuvah standing behind us. She turned again to look at the fleeing figure, but he had already disappeared. She closed her mouth on her words, and nodded her head understandingly.

"This is my Aunt Ahuvah," Shoshi introduced us. "Aunt Ahuvah married my mother's brother Jake."

I knew the situation was causing awkwardness, so I just smiled and put my hand out politely. Aunt Ahuvah smiled in return and shook my hand.

I'm sure, now, you are all perplexed as to what was unconventional about this aunt. Aunt Ahuvah was wearing a black sheitel, styled so it softly framed her small face. Her skin was very light, and she looked exactly like a China doll. That's right. You understood me correctly. I did say China doll.

We walked into the house and were greeted by a hubbub of activity. It seemed as if cousins were coming out of every crack and every door. We were introduced to everyone, but all the faces were a big blur. All, that is, except Aunt Ahuvah's. I couldn't wait to hear the story of her life.

Sara walked beside me. The smile on her face seemed painted on. I could see her thoughts were elsewhere. Was she also trying to figure out where Aunt Ahuvah was from?

Judy saw us standing at the side, and as she walked into the dining room, she casually called to me, "Did you pick up your package, Bracha?"

I looked around for the traces of a package, but I couldn't find any.

"What package?" I asked my cousin.

Judy led me to the breakfront in the dining room. First she searched one shelf, expecting to find the package. When it wasn't there, she began searching the other shelves.

"That's funny," she said. "I'm sure I put it right here."

Judy looked all over the breakfront. "I purposely put the package in the breakfront for safekeeping," she said, more to herself than to her guests. "There's only family here. Who would expect it to disappear so easily?"

"Don't worry," I told her. "I'm not expecting any package. It's probably not very important."

Judy froze as she realized the package really wasn't there.

There was a stricken look on her face.

"Oh, but Bracha, it's important."

Judy paused.

"We had better call Detective Solomon," she said quietly. "The package held a very expensive antique Oriental jade jewel direct from China. It arrived here by special delivery. You were supposed to deliver it straight to your father."

I stood silently as I realized the enormity of the situation.

I then looked at Sara, and as we both remembered the fleeing figure, we turned toward Shoshi. Shoshi was standing at Aunt Ahuvah's side. As our eyes shifted toward Aunt Ahuvah, we were surprised to see her eyes glistening with tears as she shook her head in denial. Supporting Aunt Ahuvah, Shoshi led us into the kitchen.

We all sat down at the edge of our chairs as Judy went to call Detective Solomon. I couldn't understand why Aunt Ahuvah was crying, but as I turned toward Sara, she signaled both Shoshi and me to follow her. We went upstairs to the room Sara and I shared, and sat down on the beds.

"Do you know why I called you up here?" Sara began.

We shook our heads in the negative.

"I figured you didn't," she explained. "But I have the proof in my camera."

"I don't know what you're talking about." I looked at Sara. "Will you please explain and stop looking at us so deviously?"

"Well," Sara continued. "While you were being thrown

about on the threshold of the Friedman house, I took a picture of your attacker."

She smiled mischievously, yet with a slightly puzzled frown.

"And your attacker," she continued, "who, by the way, was probably running away because he stole your father's valuable package, was none other than..."

And this time she paused dramatically.

"Than our Asian follower."

"No!" I said with surprise.

"No," Shoshi said at the same time, but in denial.

"Yes." Sara nodded, convinced.

"Then if you're so sure..." Shoshi began.

"Yes." Sara nodded again.

"Then," Shoshi concluded, "we have a real problem on our hands."

"Why is that?" I asked.

"Because," Shoshi said. "Because I know the guy who ran out of my house. His name is Charlie, or Chaim. And he's my Aunt Ahuvah's brother."

Sara and I waited. We wanted to ask Shoshi to explain to us about her Aunt Ahuvah, but we found it very awkward to ask. Shoshi, however, helped us along.

"You're probably wondering about my Aunt Ahuvah," Shoshi said.

We nodded our heads, relieved.

"Aunt Ahuvah was raised in Chinatown as a Buddhist," Shoshi explained. "She was always very uncomfortable with the religion, and started searching among the other religions of the world.

"About ten years ago, she converted to Judaism, but not according to halachah. When my Uncle Jake was in college, he met Aunt Ahuvah. At that point Aunt Ahuvah realized her conversion hadn't been done properly, and she asked Uncle Jake to please guide her to the proper authorities so she could be considered a Jewess according to halachah. Uncle Jake introduced her to a real *beis din*. Now comes the most interesting part of the story.

"The *beis din* ruled that Aunt Ahuvah didn't have to be converted."

"What?" Sara and I both exclaimed at once.

"That's right." Shoshi nodded her head as she enjoyed the surprised reaction.

"The *beis din* questioned Aunt Ahuvah as to why she wished to convert. She described her search for the true religion, and then as an afterthought, Aunt Ahuvah added an interesting statement.

"She said, 'Anyhow, my great-grandmother was Jewish.'

"The way Aunt Ahuvah described it, her great-grandmother was from an assimilated family who moved to China as merchants before the turn of the century. Her great-grandmother, in turn, married into the Chinese Jewish community in Shanghai. That community was also assimilated and not observant. Aunt Ahuvah's great-grandparents moved to San Francisco, and her whole family was raised in Chinatown. The *beis din* then proclaimed that Ahuvah didn't have to convert because she's accepted as a Jewish daughter of Israel from birth."

"But I don't understand," I said, puzzled. "Was there really a Chinese Jewish community? Were they really Jewish?"

"Yes." Shoshi nodded. "They even had a shul. They originated in China many hundreds of years ago. And when there was a large immigration of Chinese to America during the 1800s, a small Jewish group also settled in San Francisco."

"So your Aunt Ahuvah is really Jewish from birth," I mused.

"But what's with this Charlie-Chaim?" Sara queried. "How does he get into the story?"

"Chaim is about your age. Up until he was bar mitzvah age, he just ignored his heritage and acted like a typical Chinese teenager. Then, when he turned thirteen, he realized that perhaps he should stop denying his heritage and accept the responsibilities of a Jewish adult. Then the fireworks erupted. Things went completely out of hand."

We were sitting entranced by Shoshi's story.

"They say it's not unusual for teenagers to be mixed up and have to search to find themselves."

Sara and I exchanged glances and began to giggle. Shoshi also started to laugh. We always thought *we* were the most misunderstood teenagers.

"Well, Chaim is even more mixed up than is typical," Shoshi explained. "He grew up in Chinatown among Chinese Buddhists. And then his sister drops this bombshell that he's really Jewish. And then his mother accepts his sister and agrees that they're Jewish but continues to conduct her life as typical Chinese. But to top it all off, he got involved with gangs. He runs away from home for weeks at a time, and then when he comes home, he's always so penitent."

Sara looked at both of us and nodded her head.

"Then it could have definitely been Chaim following us in Pineville," she said.

"But is he actually capable of stealing my father's jewel?" I asked.

Shoshi shook her head negatively.

"I don't know," she answered. "I really don't know."

10

SIMCHAH AT PEBBLE BEACH

We had gone to bed that evening just a little subdued. All during supper, Barry, a tall muscular man, tried to divert our attention from the missing jewel. He continuously joked. Menachem, the typical teenage investigator, was spouting all sorts of unusual theories and conclusions.

Sara, who saw spies and intelligence agents hidden under every stone, fit in with the active imaginations of the rest of the family. She was enjoying herself immensely.

After supper, Detective Solomon came to ask us some questions. We couldn't really help him with his investigation because we had never even seen the jewel or its package. He had, of course, notified my father of the theft, and my father said he would fax a picture of the jewel when he got to his office in the morning.

But I was plain scared. I tried not to show it in front of Sara. As we went to bed that evening, though, I knew I hadn't fooled her.

"Don't worry," she reassured me. "Nothing serious is going to happen. They'll find your father's jewel, and everything will be all right.

"I'm glad we didn't tell Detective Solomon about our suspicions of Chaim," she added as an afterthought. "Maybe if we can confront Chaim ourselves, we'll be able to help him find his true self — his Jewish self."

Although Sara's statement was said with determination, I felt it lacked conviction.

"I hope you're right," I said with a yawn. "I hope you're right."

We packed our suitcases for the trip to Pebble Beach, remembering that on Sunday we were going to go directly to Sonoma County and spend the day there. The excitement of the bar mitzvah was contagious.

Our car ride down to Pebble Beach was a mixture of hilarity and thought-provoking discussions. Our car comfortably carried Shoshi, Sara, and myself, plus my two other young cousins, Menachem and Honey.

Sara, always interested and curious and never shy, began one of the discussions with a questioning statement.

"I have lived in Pineville all of my life. My father has always either learned in the yeshivah or taught in the yeshivah. I just can't imagine the kind of life you live here in San Francisco."

Her comment was greeted with silence. I was afraid my cousins were offended. I needn't have feared.

"You know, it's funny," Shoshi began. "Before I went to Bais Yaakov of Denver, I thought all communities were like mine. I thought in each community throughout the United States there were mostly assimilated Jews and scattered families of *frum* Jews. But at Bais Yaakov, I met girls from New York and other yeshivah communities. Then I knew that our family situation was unusual."

Sara thought this over for a minute.

"Was it hard growing up as one of the only *frum* families in the community?" she asked.

"Yes," Shoshi answered without hesitation. "I always knew the way I was being raised was the proper way. I mean, all I had to do was look at my parents. There was always peace and harmony in my house. And my mother was always willing to answer all of my questions.

"But," she continued, "I always felt *different* from the rest of my friends. A lot of the kids in my class weren't even *shomer Shabbos*. I had to remember constantly that my *derech* of living was the proper way.

"*Shemiras Shabbos* was easy," Shoshi concluded. "Everyone could understand if you were *frum* there were things you couldn't do on Shabbos. Nobody even bothered to invite me to things taking place on Shabbos. I didn't even have to excuse myself. Kashrus was the same thing. But *tznius*? Well, that was a completely different subject.

"Until I was five years old, I dressed like everyone. But once I started growing older, and I had to dress in a more modest manner, I began to look different from everyone else.

"I remember," Shoshi softly said, "when I was in fifth grade, there was a heat wave in June. The temperatures hit the 90s, unusual for San Francisco. Everyone came to school without socks and wearing short sleeves. I was the only girl in knee socks and sleeves."

I visualized Shoshi standing shyly in her classroom.

"What did you do?" I asked her.

"Well, one of my friends came over to me. I think she felt sorry for me and was trying to comfort me in my predicament."

Shoshi paused and then smiled.

"She didn't realize I didn't mind dressing differently. Not only was I *proud* to be dressed like a Bais Yaakov girl, I ran home to tell my mother I was now a true *bas Yisrael*, wearing my badge of honor.

"You see," Shoshi explained, "although my grandparents are more modern than we are and really had assimilated when they had moved out West, they vividly remember the anti-Semitic war years in France. They had always infused in us a sense of pride in being Jewish. With those feelings running through my blood, could I possibly not act proud?"

Sara and I nodded. *Baruch Hashem* we didn't have to face the sacrifices Shoshi lived with daily. Could we have survived without the support of our friends? Menachem and Honey supplied us with the answer.

"Aw, Shoshi," Menachem said. "Don't be so melodramatic. You always act like a martyr."

"What do you mean?" I asked.

"Shoshi is making it sound like it's hard to grow up *frum* in a non-*frum* community," Menachem protested. "It isn't hard at all. All kids play baseball, don't they?"

I nodded as I remembered my brothers and how they taught me to play ball.

"Well, then what's the difference when you play? Boys don't care what you wear, as long as you get a hit!"

We all laughed at Menachem's straightforward answer.

"Don't forget, though, Menachem," Shoshi reminded him, "how hard it was for you when you started in Little League. At the time, the team didn't know you would be the most valuable player. Remember Daddy's battle to have you play on the team even though there were practices and games you wouldn't attend because of Shabbos?"

Menachem nodded, but continued his righteous argument.

"But look at our team now," he stated defiantly. "We're the only *shomer Shabbos* team on the West Coast. Every team member wears a yarmulke and tzitzis. Now, isn't *that* a *kiddush Hashem*?"

"I find it hard," Honey's little voice was heard coming from the corner seat. "None of my friends are *shomer Shabbos*. And they always have parties in nonkosher restaurants."

"Yes, you do have a problem." Shoshi nodded, and then she explained to us. "Honey has the bad luck of being in a class of super sophisticated seven-year-olds. The parents are professional people who are very materialistic. The girls are just offshoots of their parents. Everything is a competition. We hope things will improve next year, since the two new rabbeim who were hired both have girls Honey's age."

"I guess, although there might be rewards to living in a place like San Francisco," Sara thoughtfully concluded, "you know, being *mekarev* others and setting examples, there are also many sacrifices. What if your family wasn't so strong? What if you hadn't been proud but embarrassed? What would have happened then?"

Shoshi thought for a minute, but before she had a chance to answer, Menachem interrupted.

"We would move," he stated without leaving any room for argument.

"He's right, you know," Shoshi agreed. "Daddy sometimes described to us the way he grew up. He said he would never allow it to happen to his children. My father constantly states that the minute he sees the outside world influencing his family instead of the other way around, we would pack up and move."

"What about your father's job?" I impulsively asked.

"My grandfather asked him the same question," Shoshi stated with pride. " 'Hashem will provide,' my father answered. He's not afraid of having financial problems, because he knows Hashem will look out for us. He has complete *bitachon.*"

"In the meantime," Menachem said, "everything remains the same. Hey, is that car following us?"

Menachem's shift in conversation took us a minute to comprehend. As Shoshi looked in the rearview mirror, we all turned around and looked out of the back window.

"See that small car?" Menachem asked. "It's been behind us for a full half hour. I mean, take a look. There are so few cars on the road, he has to be following us."

Shoshi slowed the car down considerably, and at first the other car slowed also.

"See," Menachem proudly exclaimed.

Shoshi sped up, and the little car sped up, too.

"We're almost at the entrance to Seventeen Mile Drive," she said. "Let's see what happens when we get to the gate."

We slowed down at the gate, and Shoshi took out the invitation to the bar mitzvah and showed it to the gatekeeper.

"You can go through," he said.

"Sir, there is a small gray car that seems to be following us," Shoshi told the gatekeeper. "Please make sure he has a legitimate invitation. Maybe it would be advisable to take the name of the driver and check with my parents."

The gatekeeper nodded that he would follow Shoshi's instructions. We proceeded down the road, a little more relieved.

When we arrived at the hotel, we quickly went to our assigned rooms. The place was extremely luxurious. Our room windows looked out over the Pacific Ocean. The hotel was situated on a small cliff that looked down upon magnificent waves breaking on the rocks. There was a small pathway down the hill that led to a tiny cove of calm waters. A little distance off the shore were swirling tides and magnificent rocks.

"Hey, is that a seal sunning himself?" I asked Sara.

She had been busy unpacking, while I was completely engrossed in the magnificent scenery. She joined me at the window, and we stood silently in awe of the beauty outside.

"We already said a berachah on seeing the Pacific Ocean," I said. "I wonder if there's a berachah to say when you see beautiful scenery?"

"I'm sure if we would just pick up a Tehillim, we would be able to find many *perakim* that discuss the greatness and wonder of Hashem's creations."

We were interrupted by a knock on the door. When we opened up, Shoshi was standing there wearing a heavy sweater and sneakers.

"Hurry up, put on sneakers and grab a sweater," she said. "I'm going to the shoreline to watch the waves and seals for an hour or so. Come join me. And don't forget that sweater. You really need it."

We followed Shoshi's instructions and joined her at the foot of the stairs. We were just in time to greet the two detectives as they arrived. They looked extremely harried, and I wondered if there was more information that had come to light.

We greeted them with friendly smiles, but they weren't very happy to see us.

"So you're the ones," Detective Solomon accused us, standing with his suitcases in hand and chewed cigar stub grasped tightly between his teeth. His curly red hair looked more like rusty steel wool than friendly clown. He was *livid*.

"W-w-what happened?" Shoshi asked, quite daunted by Detective Solomon's brisk greeting.

Detective Solomon looked ready to explode. He couldn't verbalize what was on his mind. He gave us a frigid stare and stomped through the lobby to the hotel desk. Detective Wong was just a shadow of his partner. He, too, refused to explain anything to us.

"I wonder what's bugging those two," Sara said. "Oh, well. Who cares? Let's go and have some fun."

And so, with a shrug of our shoulders we dismissed them from our minds.

Following the stairs we had seen from the window, we slowly edged our way toward the beach. The air was crisp, and we closed our sweaters tightly. We could smell the salty sea air, and we could hear the rush of the waves. The gulls were shrieking in the air. But surrounding us was the darkness of the cypress forest that engulfed our hotel. Suddenly, as we made our last turn, the water glistened and glittered in the sunlight.

"It's like diamonds," I exclaimed.

"You're sooo original." Sara's sarcasm broke the mood.

I quickly palmed my hand in the freezing-cold water lapping at my feet and splashed Sara in her face.

Amid giggles, she attacked back. Soon, Shoshi found herself also involved, and our game became a three-way battle. After a few minutes of frolicking fun, we sat down exhausted on the sand and sunned ourselves dry.

"This place is beautiful," I said. "Can you imagine living in a house on the top of the cliff and looking out onto the ocean every single morning?"

"No," Sara answered bluntly.

"No?" both Shoshi and I asked incredulously.

"Of course not," Sara answered defiantly. And then she mischievously asked a rhetorical question. "Can you imagine how nervous my mother would be? She would constantly be counting to make sure she hadn't lost anyone."

I started to laugh while I described Sara's family to Shoshi, including all her little brothers and sisters.

"I think she would be more nervous about your brothers surfboarding in the ocean," Shoshi said.

And with that laughing comment, we dusted ourselves off from the sand and began our walk up the stairs back to the hotel.

11

BAR MITZVAH FUN

We were all sitting around many tables in the large dining room. I looked around and saw a complete assortment of different types of people adorning the Shabbos tables. I looked at everything, vividly trying to store it up in my memory so I could retell it all to my parents when I would get back home to Pineville.

First I observed the dais. Menachem was sitting uncomfortably in the center of the long table. His friends joined him at the sides. They also looked quite uncomfortable. I remembered my brothers' comments at their bar mitzvahs. Sitting in front of the whole dining room really interfered with their style. Being the center of attention meant they couldn't do anything wrong.

As I looked a little closer at Menachem's friends, I could tell they were definitely very different from Menachem and my brothers. The knitted yarmulkes were bobby-pinned to their hair. Some of the boys were even wearing their yarmulkes on the *backs* of their heads instead of the tops. They were afraid the yarmulke would mess up their hairdos.

I looked around at the various tables. Judy's and Barry's friends were unlike them. There were many women wearing short sleeves. Some women had tied scarves across their shoulders out of respect.

The men were just adult images of the boys. The hairstyles seemed uncomfortable with the black starched silk yarmulkes perched on top. Some of the men, you could tell, always covered their heads. But there were very few conservative dark suits and even fewer Shabbos hats.

Judy's family, her brothers and sisters, were all *frum*. But except for one brother, they were all much younger than Judy and only had babies. The brother who had been Barry's friend didn't even live in San Francisco. He had found it too hard and had moved to Los Angeles, which had a *frum* young crowd.

Barry stood up at the dais. Everyone quieted down to listen to his speech. It was really a *devar Torah*, and he explained the parashah in a fascinating way. Afterwards, he taught a tune to *Tzur Mishelo*. I jumped up in recognition. This was an old family tune my Zeidy in Eretz Yisrael sang. Then I laughed to myself. Of course Barry would sing that niggun. It was his Zeidy's, too.

After bentshing, which was led by Murray, we all walked out to the porch. The porch was dimly lit with soft candles in glass jars. Shoshi, Sara, and I started to walk toward the end of the porch. Suddenly, a figure loomed up in front of us. We jumped back in fright and stifled a scream.

"Sorry," Detective Solomon said. "Keep away from the edges. You never know who may be following you."

His last statement was said quite sarcastically, but we could tell he didn't mean to frighten us.

"What are you trying to say?" Sara boldly asked. "Don't you believe us? Are you accusing us of not being shadowed?"

"Well." Detective Solomon slowly looked us over. "I believed you up until today."

"W-w-what happened today?" I ventured to ask.

"Didn't Menachem tell Detective Solomon today that we were followed on the way here?" Shoshi reminded us all.

"Oh," Detective Solomon accused. "So now you're shifting the blame onto Menachem."

"We were followed," Sara insisted. "I saw the gray car myself."

Detective Solomon paused another time and began to walk away slowly. He then turned around to us one more time.

"Next time you accuse a car of following you," he said, "and insist on the gatekeeper checking out that person's credentials, do me a favor. Make sure it's not the detective who was hired to protect you, doing his job."

We all looked questioningly at each other.

"Did he say what I think he said?" Shoshi asked.

Sara began to laugh.

"I think it was Detective Solomon in the gray car we reported," she said.

"No wonder he was so frazzled when he came in!" I swallowed my laughter.

"Oh no!" We couldn't contain ourselves.

Every time we remembered Detective Solomon's harried expression when he arrived at the hotel, we began to laugh anew.

The next morning, we awakened to the sound of rushing waves on the shore. Sara opened the window and let the cold air envelop us.

"It feels so refreshing," she exclaimed. "Why can't the Atlantic Ocean be as blue and beautiful as the Pacific?"

"I'm sure there must be some beautiful coastal areas back East," I reminded Sara. "We just haven't had the opportunities to see them."

We got dressed quickly so we'd be on time for the minyan. Surprisingly enough, not only had the men arrived at nine o'clock, in time for *shacharis*, but so had most of the women. This was a very special occasion. But even so, I got the impression that shul and davening were very important to these people.

I kicked myself at my judgmental attitude. Here I was looking down at the Jewish lifestyle in San Francisco from my superior sheltered *frum* life in Pineville. Yet how many of the people I knew back home showed up at shul on time? Not only that, but I saw that everyone over here actually davened and didn't socialize. Would our *tefillah* be able to stand scrutiny compared to the sincerity of the davening of this crowd? I wondered.

Barry davened *shacharis*. His strong voice bellowed out the niggunim with strength and might. In contrast, when Menachem *leined* the parashah and the haftorah, his sweet voice flowed flawlessly. Murray then davened *mussaf*. It was a beautiful family proclamation of the victory of *frumkeit*.

I saw Judy's eyes glisten with tears as she participated in this exhibition with pride. I, too, was greatly moved.

Amid the mazal tovs, we went into the lobby for a *kiddush*. Shoshi's uncle had certainly catered a magnificent *kiddush*. All the food decorating had been left to his direction. The job was magnificent. There were swans carved out of melons. There was chopped fish in the shape of real fish.

"Boy," Sara said. "Who needs a seudah? This *kiddush* has enough food to satisfy even me."

Being that Sara is so tiny, it was indeed a funny statement.

We walked around and socialized, Shoshi introducing us to all her relatives. I was glad Shoshi was by my side and Sara was also with me. I could tell there were individuals who were staring at us. Was it because we looked different or acted different? I hoped so. I certainly didn't want to look or act like the typical American teenager of today. I began to feel the pride of being different.

Sara interpreted my thoughts exactly.

"I'm glad I got the opportunity to spend time amongst people who don't come from the same background we do," she said. "It really puts things in the proper perspective. When we're with our friends, who look and act just like we do, it's easy to forget how different we are from the rest of the world."

I nodded my head in agreement.

"Now you have a little idea of what I was talking about," Shoshi added. "You're lucky, though. In just a few days' time you'll be amongst your friends, who are just like you."

"And so will you," Sara reminded her.

"*Baruch Hashem*," Shoshi answered in a loud voice. "I'll tell you one thing, though. I don't think I would choose this type of lifestyle for my children. Give me Pineville any day."

"You're invited," Sara and I said together, in one breath, and we all started laughing.

The day progressed in a beautiful Shabbos spirit and atmosphere. It was funny, though, to see Detective Wong walking around wearing a yarmulke.

"He doesn't want to look different," Honey had whispered to Shoshi.

The melaveh malkah was simply beautiful. Everyone was dressed in their elegant best. Since it was still before Rosh Chodesh Iyar, Barry had hired a few yeshivah boys from Los Angeles to entertain the crowd. They came equipped not only with band instruments but also with a lot of *ruach*. They played all the new songs and latest music. They really added to the celebration.

Shoshi, Sara, and I put up a small *mechitzah* and began dancing in our little corner.

Before we knew it, it was two o'clock in the morning. Everybody sat quietly in their chairs while Menachem and a few of his friends got up in front of the audience. He gave a small speech, just an addition to the *pshetel* he had said at the lunch meal.

"It's usually now when the bar mitzvah bachur gets up and gives a thank-you speech," he said solemnly. "I'd like to thank everyone for coming, from my friends in school to my cousin Bracha and her friend Sara, who came all the way from Pineville, New Jersey, to share in my simchah."

I blushed in embarrassment.

"I'd like to thank my grandparents, my rebbe, my principal, and everyone else who had something to do with getting me to where I stand today."

There was a lot of applause and cheers.

"But most of all, I'd like to thank my parents. Now that I'm bar mitzvah, I'm responsible for all the mitzvos. I am also responsible for anything wrong I may do. It was with this sobering thought in mind that I composed the following song."

Menachem then gave a signal to the band. They began to play an original version of "*Shema Beni Mussar Avicha V'al Titosh Toras Imecha*," while Menachem sang and his friends harmonized.

I looked at Judy and Barry. Although they were smiling, tears were flowing from their eyes. I looked at the rest of the guests. They, too, were crying. I wasn't surprised to find my cheeks wet with tears at Menachem's beautiful proclamation of love for his parents and devotion to the mitzvos of Hashem.

12

MISSING

We woke up at eleven the next morning, davened, ate breakfast, and packed. Most of the guests had already left for San Francisco. We had about a three-hour journey ahead of us, so we hastily threw everything into our suitcases. By twelve thirty, we were standing near the car, ready to leave.

"Is Menachem in the car?" Shoshi called from the front steps of the hotel.

Sara and I rechecked the car in case he had sneaked inside when we weren't looking.

"No," I called back. "Only Honey and us."

Judy joined Shoshi on the porch. She looked harried

and frazzled. Detective Solomon came out of the hotel and also joined the group.

In a few minutes, Shoshi came down the stairs. Gone was the bounciness I was beginning to associate with her. She seemed a little depressed.

"Is something the matter?" Sara asked. "Is Menachem missing?"

"I don't know," Shoshi answered. "We're not really sure. The last hour has been so mixed up, with people leaving and different carpool arrangements being planned. Mommy thinks Menachem might have gone ahead with my grandfather."

"Is there any way to reach him on the road?" I questioned softly.

"No." Shoshi shook her head. "We've always talked about getting a car phone. But Daddy insists that when he's driving he doesn't want to be interrupted with business calls. That's the chance he gets to listen to his Torah tapes. And my grandfather is using Daddy's car."

"So what are we going to do?" Sara asked.

"My mother told me to go ahead," Shoshi answered. "She'll stick around for about another half hour. Detective Solomon said we should all meet at the house in Sonoma."

We all quietly settled into the car. The drive up to Sonoma was very subdued. At first we gave suggestions as to where Menachem could be. But always in the back of our minds, we were afraid this might have something to do with my father's stolen jewel. What could Menachem possibly have to do with the stealing of the precious gem?

"I really don't get the connection," I commented quietly to Sara in the back seat of the car. "If they already stole my father's valuable jewel, why should anybody try to kidnap Menachem?"

"And why Menachem?" Sara asked me back. "If someone should be kidnapped, it should really be you, Bracha. After all, it's *your* father's jewel."

Her statement didn't make me feel too comfortable, and I was glad we were whispering and Shoshi wouldn't be able to overhear us. But I was wrong. She had heard.

"More than that," Shoshi contributed her viewpoint. "Maybe if Menachem was really kidnapped, it has nothing whatsoever to do with your father's jewel. Maybe the jewel being stolen was just coincidental. After all, my father has been receiving threatening phone calls, and there has been some vandalism at the winery."

The rest of the journey was filled with silence as we contemplated the reasons behind the actions.

When we arrived at the vineyard, Murray and Ruthy were already there. Barry, we were told, was at the wine factory taking care of some business. Soon Judy and Detectives Solomon and Wong appeared in their police car. We all sat around in the small living room and awaited Barry's arrival.

The living room was tastefully decorated in soft earthy tones. The furniture was of high-quality leather, soft and supple from use. The oriental carpet was meticulously clean. All the wooden furniture shone with polish. This was a room lovingly cared for, and it reflected happy times. As we sat waiting for Barry, we felt that any new information would intrude like an ominous black cloud.

We heard the squeak of the brakes as Barry's car stopped short and splattered the gravel in the driveway. The door opened, and we heard his heavy footsteps in the hallway. Barry entered the room, his hand clutching a piece of paper and his face reflecting the sad news it brought. He looked as if he had aged ten years since I had seen him last night.

Judy got up from the edge of the chair where she had been sitting, anxiously awaiting her husband. Barry slowly walked over to her.

"Menachem?" she questioned.

Barry shook his head ever so slightly.

"Menachem's been kidnapped," he answered.

The color completely drained out of Judy's face. She collapsed in the chair behind her, and her hands started to visibly shake. Up until this point we had only suspected that Menachem had been kidnapped. Now Barry was bringing proof of the truth.

Shoshi hurriedly ran into the kitchen and brought back a cup of ice-cold water, which she handed to her mother. All eyes turned to Detective Solomon as he read the note Barry had handed him.

Judy sat up straight in her chair and took a deep breath. She seemed to gain control of herself.

"What does the note say?" Judy asked Detective Solomon.

The detective looked at Barry to gauge the amount of information Judy would be able to take. Barry nodded and stood behind Judy's chair.

"The note says that Menachem has been taken as a hostage," Detective Solomon revealed. "As soon as Barry follows the forthcoming instructions, Menachem will be released unharmed."

In the meantime, Detective Wong had been on the telephone, instructing headquarters to place a tracer on all incoming phone calls. Within an hour, the house was buzzing with police activity. The original circle of people who had been in the living room remained in their same positions. Finally, Sara motioned that I should follow her.

We went into another room, obviously the dining room, and stood looking outside the large picture windows. Surprisingly, the sun was still shining on the vineyard and the fields. And everything was so bleak inside.

"Do you think we should daven or say some *tehillim*?" Sara asked.

"I don't know," I answered. "I wish my father was here. He always knows what to do in an emergency."

Before we had a chance to make any decisions, the telephone rang in the living room. We rushed back to see everyone frozen in their spot. Ruthy's hand was holding the cup of coffee she had been about to sip. Even Judy's tissues, which she had been incessantly wringing in her hands, were frozen. After three rings, when Detective Solomon had completed activating some dials on his equipment, Barry answered the telephone. We could hear the conversation.

"Hello," Barry said.

There was a muffled and quick response.

"We have your precious son. You have something precious of ours. Meet me in your office at the winery. No one should follow. You must come alone."

Then there was silence.

"I'm sorry," Barry said, as he held the receiver limply in his hand. "It happened too fast. What should I do?"

"Go to the winery," Detective Solomon said, "to your office. Follow their instructions, but be very hesitant and slow. Try to be clumsy. Explain to them you are worried about your son and you can't think straight or work properly. Try to get them to let you see Menachem. We'll try to observe everything from a distance."

"Can't you do something constructive?" Shoshi asked, and then she apologized. "I'm sorry, but I just don't understand what watching from a distance could do to help Daddy. They could kidnap him just as easily."

"No," Detective Solomon reassured her. "They aren't out to kidnap anyone else. Menachem was taken as a *hostage*. They said we have something precious they want. We must find out what this object is and arrange a trade. Then they'll return Menachem safely. At this point we have no choice but to follow their instructions." Shoshi just stood in her place. She probably understood there were complex reasons. She just wasn't ready to accept them.

Barry and the two detectives went outside. Detective Wong stuck a device underneath Barry's front fender to keep a trace on the car. Barry started the motor and left. The two detectives followed in their car. The rest of the law enforcement officers stayed behind, each busy with his own specialty.

I was very concerned about Honey. From the moment Menachem had been kidnapped, she hadn't said a word. We had tried coaxing her into some conversation in the car, but she refused to cooperate.

When we had arrived at the house, she sat herself down in the corner and began playing with her dolls. I moved a little closer to her, if only to cuddle her. I was watching her, but I wasn't really paying attention to what she was saying. Finally I realized that Honey was playacting an incident that must have really happened. She was pretending one of her dolls was Menachem.

I listened more attentively and signaled to Sara and Shoshi to quietly move closer and to be alert.

Honey picked up one doll and said in a perfect imitation of Menachem's voice, "You stay right over here, Honey. I don't want you to come with me. I am going exploring near the edge of the cliff, which can be very dangerous. We'll be going to Sonoma soon, so be a good girl and wait at the hotel."

Then Honey moved the doll in her right hand, the Menachem doll, a little away. She then used her own voice to speak for the doll in her left hand.

"Boy, Menachem is some big shot. Just because he's bar mitzvah, he thinks he can boss me around. Well, I'll show him."

Honey then moved her left-hand doll, the one she was depicting as herself, and let it secretly follow her Menachem doll.

Honey hid the Honey doll behind the leg of a chair. She

then picked up two other dolls and had them walk sneakily to where the Menachem doll was standing.

Suddenly, the two new dolls pounced on the Menachem doll.

"I've got him," one doll said in a gruff voice.

"Let me go," the Menachem doll said in a loud voice.

Honey continued playing with the dolls, having them hold the Menachem doll tightly. The Menachem doll soon stopped moving, and the other two dolls carried it away.

We thought Honey's little play was finished. We were just about to interrupt her, when we heard her say in the same gruff voice of the gangster, "You go on to meet Chin in Sonoma. I'm taking the kid back to Grant."

At that point, Honey put down all the dolls. She then picked up the doll that had played the part of Honey. The Honey doll began to cry.

The three of us exchanged looks. Honey had witnessed the whole kidnapping and had just replayed it for us with her dolls. No wonder she hadn't said a word in the car. She must have been so upset.

Shoshi signaled us to follow her into the dining room.

"I wonder," she said, "if Honey actually saw the kidnappers."

"If so," Sara responded excitedly, "then she'd be able to recognize them and help capture them."

I shook my head.

"Not only that," I said with distress, "but if she can recognize them, then probably she'd be able to identify them. She could be in a lot of danger."

"You're right," Sara and Shoshi admitted.

We discussed our new information. We decided we would keep a close watch over Honey and not let her out of our sight. At the same time, when Detective Solomon would return, we would reveal everything to him.

We returned to the living room, and it was as if we had never left. Everyone was still in the same position. Even Honey was still sitting in the corner, playing with her dolls. Now she was reenacting the bar mitzvah.

"That's much safer ground," Sara said.

We all agreed.

13

A GLITTERING CONFESSION

Barry's car pulled up into the driveway, and Detective Solomon's unmarked car sped up right behind him. They walked into the house together, but no conversation had passed between them.

"What happened?" Murray was the first to ask.

"I think we had better sit down. We have a major problem on our hands," Barry answered.

"Wait one minute," Detective Solomon said, "while I activate this recorder. Now, begin telling us everything that happened from the moment you left this room, until this moment when you arrived back."

"Well," Barry began, pacing slowly back and forth. "I

drove up to the winery gate. Our whole property is surrounded by a locked gate to discourage trespassers. Having a kosher winery requires more stringent security. I deactivated the alarm on the gate. I pulled the car in and left the gate open so Detective Solomon could follow quietly if he so wished.

"I then deactivated the alarm on the front door and unlocked it. I entered the building and left all alarms and locks open. I unlocked my office door in the bottling department, sat down at my desk and waited. After fifteen minutes, when I saw there was nobody joining me, I took a short walk around the building. Nothing seemed to be disturbed. At one point I thought I heard a noise in the storage room, but when I inspected it, that room also seemed undisturbed. No machinery was turned on. All the wine was sealed with my special kashrus seal.

"After returning to my office, I noticed this on my desk. I opened the envelope and read the note. I then locked up everything and reactivated all alarms. I don't understand."

"What don't you understand?" Detective Solomon asked patiently.

Barry looked greatly perplexed.

"How did that note get on my desk? With all my security, how was someone able to get in?"

Detective Solomon was about to say something when the sound of the ringing telephone pierced the air. Detective Solomon pressed the button for the tracer to operate, and Barry answered the telephone.

"Hello," he said.

"Thank you," the same muffled voice hurriedly spoke. "I hope you have received our little note."

"Where is my son?" Barry asked anxiously. "Where's Menachem?"

"He is well."

"When will you release him?" Barry persisted, as Detective Solomon pantomimed that he should continue talking. "You promised you would free him!"

"At the right time," was the answer. "First, though, you must fulfill your part of the bargain. You have forty-eight hours. By five o'clock Tuesday afternoon, we must have the merchandise. And *then* you will see your son." At the conclusion of that statement, there was silence on the line.

"Did Barry speak long enough?" Judy asked nervously.

"I'll find out in a minute," Detective Solomon answered.

Almost as soon as he finished speaking, the telephone rang again. Detective Solomon indicated that Barry should answer it. He did, and immediately handed the telephone to Detective Solomon. The detective grunted a few times and scribbled a few numbers on his pad.

"I thought so," he mumbled.

We all waited for Detective Solomon to enlighten us. He chewed on his cigar butt noiselessly.

"We were able to get the first three digits of the phone number," Detective Solomon explained. "The numbers are 434. That indicates the phone call came from the San Francisco area. I think we had better move our operations back to San Francisco. Let's see what the merchandise is. Now, let me read that note."

Detective Solomon handled the note gingerly and read it aloud. It was composed of words cut out from magazines.

Exchange the boy for Oriental Jewel. Place in locker #178 in Greyhound Terminal, San Francisco.

"I don't understand," Judy said. "Is he referring to Bracha's jewel?"

Barry nodded.

"I think so," he said. There was a long moment of silence as we realized the hopelessness of the situation.

"But we don't have the jewel," Judy said in a small voice.

We all stood frozen, even more frightened than before.

"Maybe I could help you," said a voice from the door.

We all turned toward the door, as if pulled magnetically to the voice.

Chaim, Ahuvah's brother, was standing in the threshold of the open doorway, silhouetted against the setting sun. He took a step forward into the room and extended his closed hand. As he opened his fingers, we all saw the most magnificent jewel sitting in the palm of his hand. It was a small, oval-shaped, perfect Imperial Jade surrounded by the most beautiful clear-cut glittering diamonds.

"So you did steal it," Sara exclaimed triumphantly.

Chaim nodded his head.

"I don't want to bring additional trouble to you, but may I explain?" he asked apologetically.

We all nodded and sat down quietly in the living room.

Chaim took off the baseball cap he was wearing, and we were surprised to see a yarmulke on his head.

"A little over a year ago," Chaim began to explain, "before I was bar mitzvah, I got mixed up with some gangs in school. Everyone belongs to a gang, which is ruled by different Tongs."

Chaim saw we weren't quite following his conversation, so he explained with a little more detail for us.

"Tongs are Chinese societies. They do some good for the community, but they're also associated with force and criminal activities."

Chaim paused, and I could see he was intimidated by the detectives sitting around, listening to his explanation.

Detective Wong continued. "Chaim is right," he said. "In the police force, we refer to the Tongs as the Chinese Mafia."

"Nowadays the Tongs don't act as the strong men," Chaim continued. "The gangs do all the dirty work. We don't mind, as this is a sign of strength and bravery.

"That, of course, was my attitude before my bar mitzvah. Afterwards, though, I found it hard to be an active gang member and also an observant Jew."

Chaim hesitated. He looked at Ahuvah apologetically.

"That's why I kept on running away. Whenever the *dai low*, the leader of our gang, literally the 'elder brother,' wished me to do a criminal act, I'd try to escape."

Chaim now looked apologetically at Sara and me.

"A few weeks ago I was sent to New York. Mr. Friedman from New York was pointed out to me in the New York Chinatown. I was told he was negotiating the purchase of a precious jewel. It was my job to see that the jewel would never get to him. I was supposed to tail him and intercept the jewel when it reached New York. That's why I followed you to the airport. I thought you were going to meet someone and receive the jewel.

"All the time I was in New York, though, I was followed. Sometimes it was by an opposing gang, and sometimes it was by the *dai low* and his cronies. There were many times I tried to escape, but I was always recaptured.

"Then the *dai low* was given notification that you girls were coming to San Francisco. He figured you were supposed to transport the jewel to your father. They knew I had access to the Friedman house through my sister, and so they wanted me to steal the jewel.

"That was what had been planned in New York." Chaim gave a bitter laugh.

"They didn't expect me to escape from their clutches at the San Francisco airport. Of course, I had a little help." Chaim nodded a thank-you to Sara and me.

"I knew they would still go about stealing the jewel, and so I stole it first to prevent the Tong from getting it."

At this point Chaim handed the jewel over to Detective Solomon.

"*Baruch Hashem,*" Judy exclaimed, relieved. "Now that we have the jewel, everything is so simple. We can exchange the jewel for Menachem. Now Menachem will be home free."

Judy didn't receive the enthusiastic response she expected. She looked at Detective Solomon, but he wouldn't meet her eyes.

Judy sat herself down again, defeated, on her chair. Detective Solomon instead addressed his response to Barry.

"It would be very simple to just exchange the jewel for Menachem," he said in a matter-of-fact tone, "but that's not the job of the police department. The criminals have given us some time to work with. Let's first try to free Menachem and capture the gangs. Maybe we'll even be lucky enough to get to the Tong involved. Chaim, we'll need your help. Come back with us, and give us all the information you can."

Although Detective Solomon was completely business-like and brusque, Chaim was hesitant to follow. Detective Solomon seemed to understand his dilemma.

"Don't worry," Detective Solomon said. "You returned the jewel, and as far as we know, you haven't committed any crimes. You're coming to help us."

A small smile began to perk up Chaim's face.

"Does this make me an amateur detective?"

Detective Solomon returned his smile and nodded.

"Before we return to San Francisco, though," Detective Solomon returned to the matter at hand, "I want to take a walk through the winery. Perhaps the thugs who left the letter accidentally left some clues."

Shoshi remembered our wish to tour the winery, and knowing the situation, she realized there wouldn't be another chance. We all piled into the cars and proceeded toward the winery.

I thought about Honey's little playacting and questioned Shoshi and Sara.

"Should we say something to Detective Solomon?" I asked as Shoshi started the car.

Shoshi shook her head.

"Maybe we should wait until we see what is uncovered in the winery," she said. "I don't think Detective Solomon has very much patience with our suggestions after the gate-keeper at Seventeen Mile Drive harassed him so much."

We all agreed.

After Barry unlocked the gate and we all filed in, Shoshi pointed to large metal containers.

"The grapes are brought into the winery in large trucks similar to dump trucks," she said. "The grapes are then stored in these containers until they're transferred to those containers, where the actual wine process is done."

We now entered the room where the wine was bottled.

"This is a job only my father, or his *shomer Shabbos* employees, are permitted to do," Shoshi stated with pride. "The wine is bottled, corked, and then sealed. If a non-Jew handles the wine at any point, it becomes *yayin nesech*, wine that a Jew isn't allowed to drink."

We listened carefully to Shoshi's descriptions and explanations. It was all very fascinating, and the vastness of the operation was astonishing.

Sara walked along the sides of the room.

"Hey, look at this," she whispered to me.

Obviously, Sara whispered because she didn't want Detective Solomon or any of his colleagues to hear her. But nothing could be put past Detective Solomon, and immediately, he was at Sara's side.

"Don't touch it," he commanded Sara.

She retreated immediately, shamefaced, because she had almost ruined some evidence. Resting in a corner, and obviously very out of place in a Jewish winery, was a sparkling green object. Using a perfectly clean handkerchief, Detective Solomon picked up the object. It was a green stone doll.

"That's a good piece of evidence, my dear," Detective Solomon saluted Sara. "This is a copy of a rare jade miniature. Chaim, does it have any significance for you?"

Chaim peered closely at the statuette. He swallowed carefully before answering and slowly nodded his head.

"This is the good luck charm carried by the Black Vultures. They're the gang that's been trying to attack me." Chaim paused. "This gang and the one I belong to, the Red Vultures, are in direct competition. My gang was assigned to get the jewel. The Black Vultures want it. The chief of the New York Tong promised us great rewards."

Chaim hesitated before he confided to Detective Solomon. "I might know where they're hiding," he said. "There's a place in Chinatown where the gang meets, and that house holds an excellent cellar. It would be a good place to hide Menachem."

Detective Solomon looked at all of us assembled around him.

"Okay," he said. "Our next stop is Chinatown."

14

SECRETS OF CHINATOWN

We had wanted to go along with the detectives, but they were quite adamant that the whole family should go home to San Francisco.

"We're also going to go to the house first and set up all our equipment," Detective Solomon said. "Then we're going to check in at the precinct. Drive carefully."

It was already night when we rolled over the Golden Gate Bridge. The lights glistened like diamonds, peeking through the fog that swirled around the bridge's towers. Even though I was still worried about Menachem, I marveled at the beauty and magnificence of the bridge's construction.

We pulled up in front of the house, totally exhausted. Seemingly in slow motion, we unpacked the car and brought our suitcases to our bedroom. Trying to keep awake, we entered the living room.

The scene that greeted us was almost the same as the one in Murray and Ruthy's house in Sonoma. Murray and Ruthy were missing, though, since they both felt they didn't have the emotional or physical strength to endure the waiting in San Francisco. They indicated they would keep in constant telephone contact through Murray and Barry's private telephone line.

Shoshi came down the stairs after putting Honey to bed. The little girl had fallen asleep in the car and had hardly stirred as Shoshi moved her to her bed.

"Detective Solomon," Shoshi said after he had completed setting up the equipment, "before you leave, we have some information to tell you."

Once Honey had fallen asleep in the car, we had discussed her doll playing. We had come to the conclusion that it was important to reveal all the information to Detective Solomon. Besides which, we felt that since Sara had redeemed us with finding the only piece of actual concrete evidence, Detective Solomon would forgive us for sending the scouts out after him for following us.

He was very interested in the information.

"Do you know who Grant is?" Sara questioned.

"I don't know who he is or who he was," Detective Solomon teased. "But I do know *where* it is. That's the main street of Chinatown."

"I guess then," I said, "Chinatown is really the place where we'll find Menachem."

"You're probably right," Detective Solomon said. "I'll check it out tomorrow."

"Why not tonight?" Shoshi questioned.

"Take a look around you," Detective Solomon said, pointing to Barry, Judy, and ourselves. "None of you people are in shape to go anywhere. We'll find nothing at night. Besides which, Chinatown seems to be their headquarters. Everything indicates it. I have to do my research tonight and feed all the information into the computer. Chaim is going to help me eliminate false leads. You people are to get a good night's sleep."

Nobody moved.

"That's an order," Detective Solomon bellowed, but it sounded more like a request.

Judy smiled wanly but didn't move from her position. We, however, followed Detective Solomon's advice. We knew he wouldn't allow us to go with him, so we had already planned to visit Chinatown ourselves on Monday morning. There wasn't that much time left before the Tuesday afternoon deadline.

I didn't sleep very comfortably that night. I kept having dreams about Menachem. I saw Honey's dolls transforming themselves into jade statuettes. At six o'clock in the morning, I felt I could permit myself to get out of bed.

I quickly washed, got dressed, and went into the living room to daven. There was no one in the room, so with as much concentration as I could muster, I davened *shacharis*. I must have been really davening with kavanah, for by the time I finished *Aleinu*, I noticed Shoshi and Sara had joined me in the room. They were also davening.

I wandered into the kitchen. Judy was sitting at the table, her eyes staring into space and her hands clutching an empty coffee cup.

"Do you want a refill?" I asked her gently.

Her eyes focused on my face, but her stare was vacant. Finally she shivered, and a light of recognition appeared in her eyes.

"I'm sorry," Judy apologized. "Did you ask me something?"

"I just wanted to get you something," I responded, unable to find the correct words to suggest my sympathetic feelings. "Is there anything you want...you need?"

Judy shook her head in the negative and continued staring into a void.

Barry then entered the room. His presence was preceded by an odor of stale smoke.

I poured myself a cup of juice and filled Judy's and Barry's cups with fresh coffee. I wished there was more I could do.

Shoshi came into the room and began making us scrambled eggs. As we ate, she explained her plan to her mother. I could see Judy was having a hard time coming to a decision. I myself reviewed the different angles. Finally, Judy reluctantly permitted us to go.

"But please, girls," she begged. "Please stay together and be very, very careful."

We quickly said our goodbyes before anyone could change their minds, and jumped into the car.

"Maybe we should take Honey along with us," Sara asked. "After all, she could probably recognize the villains."

"Don't press your luck," Shoshi advised. "Be glad we were able to escape. Let's get out of here."

We drove downtown and found a parking space right at the intersection of Grant and California. Shoshi carefully parked and went to put money into the parking meter.

"Now, isn't this *hashgachah*?" she said. "The meter is broken. We don't have to pay!"

We walked along Grant Avenue, the main thoroughfare of Chinatown. Every window displayed different Chinese artifacts and imports from China. The odors that emanated from the restaurants and food stores flavored the air with an Oriental spice. I felt like I was in a different world.

"What do we look for?" Sara asked.

"I don't know," Shoshi answered. "Jade statuettes? Rival gangs? Red and black vultures?"

Sara and I giggled.

"Let's just look for all of the above," I suggested.

"Yes," Sara agreed. "But let's especially keep an eye out for Menachem."

We continued strolling the streets, peering into the windows and observing all the activity.

"Let's just go into each store and pretend we're shopping," Sara suggested. "Maybe we'll be able to pick up some information by listening closely to conversations."

We walked into the next store. It was a three-floor shop: basement, main floor, and upper level. We started with the basement.

"Wow, look at all these antiques," Sara stated. "This must be worth a fortune."

I poked Sara in the ribs.

"Please whisper," I told her. "You're embarrassing me."

"I know," Sara answered. "I can tell. Your face is all red."

That, of course, made me blush even more.

As we talked, we walked along the aisles. Of course, this store was so crowded there was almost no room between the piles of merchandise. We barely managed to squeeze through.

"Hey, look over there." I poked both Shoshi and Sara and pointed to a locked glass case.

A Chinese woman saw my gesture and came over to me.

"Would you like to see some jade?" she asked politely.

We shook our heads.

"I don't think I can afford any of this," I told her. "But it is really beautiful."

We continued walking down the aisle and saw some more jade locked behind glass doors.

"Hey, there are little jade dolls," Sara whispered.

Sure enough, on one of the shelves was a row of tiny jade statuettes. Each one was a little different from the other.

The Chinese woman noticed we had paused at that display case and returned to explain the contents to us.

"These are very valuable antiques," she said. "They have great powers and cost a lot of money. A person who purchases one of these will be blessed with great riches and fortune."

She then walked away to help another customer.

"I never thought I would actually see a real *avodah za-rah*," Sara said. "I think she actually believes those little statues have such a great power. It's ridiculous."

"I wonder if the gangs purchase their statuettes in this store," I said thoughtfully.

We stayed in that store for over an hour, waiting to see if anyone would come in and show an interest in purchasing a jade statuette.

"Let's try another store," Sara suggested, depressed.

We followed her advice and searched about ten stores. There were stores that sold Chinese linen, and stores that sold Chinese souvenirs. There were many stores that sold jade statuettes. But we couldn't find anyone purchasing a statuette.

Suddenly, Sara stopped.

"What's the matter?" I asked.

"I can't believe it," she said.

"Can't believe what?" Shoshi asked.

"Listen," Sara suggested.

We stood and listened to the voices coming from the camera store in front of which we were standing.

"That is so out of place," Sara stated, laughing.

We all laughed as we looked into the store. Standing behind the counter were obviously the owners. They had black curly hair and dark complexions. They were certainly not Asian, and they were speaking about their merchandise in a foreign tongue. Why were we laughing? Because who would expect the owners of a camera shop right in the middle of Chinatown to be Israelis speaking Hebrew?

We continued searching for some clue.

"I'm starved," Sara said.

"You're always hungry," I answered.

"Well, this time," Shoshi said, "we can at least go to my uncle's restaurant and have some lunch."

We walked back to the car, continuously aware of our surroundings, hoping we would see some hint of Menachem or his kidnappers. But we didn't have any luck.

We arrived at the car and settled in while Shoshi started the motor. She then took us to her uncle's store, a trip of about a half hour. We ate some sandwiches and marveled at all the food supplies he had for sale.

"There's even *chalav Yisrael* ice cream," I exclaimed in delight.

We packed a nosh bag and proceeded back to Chinatown. Invigorated by the good food, we were a little more optimistic.

Arriving in the Chinatown area, Shoshi drove directly to the spot where we had parked that morning.

"It's taken," she said. "I knew someone would grab it as soon as we would pull away. Oh, well. Let's find another parking space."

We found another spot pretty quickly on the next block, Sacramento, also right off of Grant. Shoshi took out some change to feed the parking meter.

"Well, look who's here," came a familiar voice behind us. We quickly turned around.

Detective Solomon was standing at the rear of Shoshi's car, his foot resting on the bumper.

"You're not *spying*, are you?" Detective Solomon asked, sarcastically.

I began to blush for a change.

"Sometimes, we don't do too badly," Sara reminded him.

"Good answer," Detective Solomon saluted her. "Just be careful, girls."

He then went on his way.

"Should we follow him?" Shoshi asked.

"Maybe it's not such a bad idea," I agreed, always the insecure one looking for protection by the police force.

"It's a great idea," Sara said excitedly. "Maybe we'll get to see the actual capture of the criminals."

We kept a close watch on Detective Solomon up ahead. He blended in quite easily with the crowd. He was dressed as a typical tourist, very casually.

As we walked along Grant Avenue, following Detective Solomon, we still were constantly observing the stores and the people around us.

Suddenly, Shoshi froze. We all saw it at the same time.

Detective Solomon was walking about fifteen feet ahead of us. There was a constant flow of pedestrian traffic in between us and him. We were just about to pass a Chinese restaurant, an area Detective Solomon had walked by and dismissed. We heard a screech of brakes and saw a car pull up. In the amount of time it takes to tell, four swarthy Chinese individuals got out of the car. Half-carrying a fifth person, they proceeded into the Chinese restaurant. What made us freeze?

The fifth person, the one the men were half-carrying into the restaurant, was a young boy wearing a yarmulke.

The boy was partially blocked from view by his companions, and we couldn't see his face, but after all, he *was* wearing a yarmulke.

Could it be? Was it Menachem?

15

CAPTURED AT LAST

We didn't want to call attention to ourselves. We knew that someone, possibly Menachem, had been taken forcibly inside the restaurant. We had to get Detective Solomon's attention quickly without calling attention to ourselves.

I was frozen to the spot with indecision. It's a good thing Sara is such a fast thinker. As the door closed behind the criminals, Sara had already reached Detective Solomon. He hurriedly came back with her.

"What did you see?" he demanded quickly, as he guided us to a spot across the street.

We described the scene exactly to him.

His shoulders released their tight muscular grip symbolic of his getting ready for action.

"I'm sorry," he said, obviously disappointed. "But your information isn't enough to use for a search warrant."

"Why not?" Sara asked.

"There is no proof that anything suspicious just occurred," he explained.

"No proof?" Shoshi questioned in surprise. "But we just described to you how four people actually half-carried a fifth individual into the restaurant."

"Maybe the fifth person was ill," Detective Solomon patiently explained. "Maybe he was weak from hunger. After all, it's a restaurant. There's no reason to assume the five individuals weren't just going in for some lunch."

"But these weren't any five people," Sara tried to explain. "There's no way that all five people will be eating lunch in the Chinese restaurant."

"Why not?" Detective Solomon asked. "What's wrong with eating lunch in a Chinese restaurant?"

"Because," I explained patiently. "Nobody wearing a yarmulke would eat a nonkosher lunch in a Chinese restaurant."

These words were a quick stimulus for action. Detective Solomon took out his walkie talkie, and suddenly there was a great flurry of activity in front of the restaurant. None of these individuals were in uniform, but each in their own way seemed quite adept and astute.

"Now, you girls are to steer clear of everything," Detective Solomon warned us. "Do you hear?"

We all nodded our heads. I was glad Detective Solomon

had given us this sage advice. I just knew Sara was wishing she could be in the center of the action.

The detectives entered the Chinese restaurant, two or three at a time. We waited outside, across the street, for about fifteen minutes.

"Do you think perhaps we missed all the action?" Sara asked.

"I hope so," I mumbled to myself.

"I wonder what's happening in there," Shoshi said, worriedly. "I hope it was Menachem, and he's okay."

The sun was shining, and the streets were crowded with people. Everyone was going about his own private business. Two teenagers were listening to music on a radio. A little girl was chasing her brother and crying. The whole world seemed oblivious to the drama taking place inside the Chinese restaurant.

"Hey," Sara exclaimed. "Isn't that the same car that brought Menachem and the gang to the restaurant?"

The small black car had slowly drawn to a stop in front of the entrance to the restaurant.

"We've got to do something," Shoshi said. "They're going to use that car as an escape vehicle for a quick getaway."

"Didn't Detective Solomon warn us not to get involved?" I reminded them.

We stood there, anxiously watching the car, waiting for the criminals to come out of the restaurant.

We obviously weren't the only people beginning to be concerned. The driver of the car was also getting nervous. He got out of the car, leaving the engine running. He looked at his watch and then at the second floor. Was he waiting for some signal?

He seemed not to be able to wait any longer, and without stopping the running engine, he slammed the car door and ran into the restaurant.

"Now's our chance," Sara cried to Shoshi. "Quickly, jump into the car and drive off somewhere and park it far away."

Sara's words were like a command. Without even daring to think of the consequences, Shoshi leaped into the car, and with a squeal of brakes took a turn at the corner.

"Are you nuts?" I asked Sara in shock. "Do you know that if it's not the kidnappers' car, Shoshi can be arrested for theft?"

Sara looked at me in surprise.

"I-I-I didn't think," she stammered. "I hope I didn't get Shoshi into trouble."

We stayed in our positions across the street from the Chinese restaurant. Suddenly, the door opened, and three men came running out. One was the driver of the car. He froze in shock when he saw the car wasn't there.

That minute of indecision, while the criminal stood in one place looking for his car, was enough time for a detective to follow him out of the building and handcuff him.

But where had the other two men gone?

I saw one begin to cross the street. It looked like he was coming directly to Sara and me. He was obviously not looking for us but rather for a means of escape. I saw Detective Solomon emerge from the building.

Sara and I exchanged glances.

In one movement, we both stuck out a foot and tripped the man. He went sprawling on the floor. All that remained for Detective Solomon to do was handcuff him.

And the third criminal? Where was he? He had made a left turn out of the building and was about to cross the street. He didn't count on Shoshi coming back in her car, though.

She arrived just in time to screech to a stop and block his exit. Detective Wong then proceeded to handcuff him.

Things were in a turmoil then for about fifteen minutes as police cars arrived and took all the prisoners away. I wanted to ask Detective Solomon what had happened with Menachem. He was busy, though, taking care of police business.

Finally, all the prisoners were handcuffed and sent down to the precinct to be questioned. The activity abated slightly, and Detective Solomon finally acknowledged our presence.

"Where's Menachem?" Shoshi asked anxiously.

"He's okay," Detective Solomon answered. "He's lying down in a room upstairs under police surveillance. Your parents should be arriving shortly, and then we'll all go over to the precinct. I need a detailed report from Menachem, and a report from you three, too. You did a very good detective job today."

I don't know about the others, but I was certainly blushing from embarrassment.

"By the way," Sara asked Shoshi. "What did you do with the little black car?"

"Oh." Shoshi shrugged. "I couldn't find a parking space, so I parked the car in our parking space, and brought my car instead."

She paused for a minute.

"He might get a ticket," she said. "Or he might even be towed away. There was no time left on the meter, and I didn't have any more change."

16

CELEBRATION

That Monday evening, when we all were sitting around the dining room table, the feelings of the family were euphoric.

Honey kept on approaching Menachem and touching his sleeve. She wanted to make sure he was really home. It's strange how, once Menachem was freed and we were all rejoicing, we forgot the worry and the tension we had recently lived through. We only spoke excitedly about the mystery involved, and we conveniently forgot all about the danger.

But while all of us young people had forgotten about how scared we'd been, the adults hadn't. You could really see the agony and emotional turmoil Judy and Barry had been subjected to. The lines of worry on their faces were permanently etched into their features.

Menachem, though, was relating his experiences with an easy disregard to the danger.

"Weren't you scared?" I asked him.

"Scared?" Menachem scoffed, acting really macho. "Scared of what? They wouldn't have harmed a hair on my head."

"No?" Shoshi questioned quietly. "That's not the way Chaim tells it. Those gangs never release anyone unharmed."

Menachem didn't have an answer. I was afraid my imagination was being a little too active. I didn't want to voice my thoughts, but the truth was, I didn't think the kidnappers had any plans of releasing Menachem.

"Isn't there a special berachah I'm supposed to say?" Menachem asked, as he seemed to recall the danger he had been in. "Isn't there something I'm supposed to say because I was in prison?"

"On Thursday," Barry answered, "during *krias haTorah*, you'll bentsh *gomel*."

"Well, I know what I'm going to say," Sara said. "*Baruch Hashem* you're home."

And we all answered, "Amen," solemnly and seriously.

Judy then turned to us. She hadn't taken her eyes off Menachem since she first saw him.

"What made you send Detective Solomon into the restaurant?" she asked. "Did you actually see the men taking him in?"

"Well, yes and no," Sara answered in a puzzle.

Barry raised his eyebrows and requested some clarification.

"It all happened very fast," I started to say.

"You see," Shoshi continued. "A car pulled up in front of the Chinese restaurant. It just happened to pull up right after Detective Solomon had passed by the restaurant and right before we were going to pass it."

"It didn't just happen to pull up at that moment," Sara reminded everyone. "It was completely *hashgachah*."

"For sure," Shoshi continued. "Just think what could have happened had Detective Solomon requested that we walk *with* him. We would have missed the car completely!"

"There were six occupants in the car," I continued the story. "It all happened very fast. We saw four people get out of the car and kind of drag or help the fifth person in the car."

"That was because," Menachem interrupted, "when I was in the car I pretended to be asleep. I figured when the car would stop, I'd make my escape. At first they'd hidden me in a dark cellar. I tried to run away once from the cellar, so I guess they weren't going to take any chances while walking into the restaurant. Those four guys were so strong, I wasn't able to go any place except where they directed me."

"Anyhow," Sara went on, "when the five individuals walked the short distance out of the car and into the restaurant, we knew one of those people would *never* willingly go into a Chinese restaurant."

"I don't understand," Ruthy said. She and Murray had arrived to help celebrate. "Why *wouldn't* he go into a restaurant?"

"Because," I triumphantly explained our conclusive evidence of foul play, "the fifth person was wearing a yarmulke! No *frum* Jew wearing a yarmulke would enter a Chinese restaurant."

"Good thinking," Menachem said. "Ready to start a detective agency?"

We all laughed at Menachem's joke, except Sara.

"Sara," I warned her. "That was a joke! You're not seriously thinking of becoming a detective?"

"Just think," her eyes glistened as she looked toward a dream. "The Sara and Bracha Detective Duo."

Just then, we were interrupted by the doorbell's ring.

Shoshi got up to answer it. In walked Detective Solomon and Detective Wong. We made room at the dining room table. As Detective Solomon placed his crushed silk yarmulke on his head, Honey ran to bring him a piece of cake.

"I'm going to make sure I wear this thing every time I eat," he said, pointing to his yarmulke. "This yarmulke here helped me find Menachem. I won't forget that piece of news so quickly."

He removed his ever-present cigar butt from his mouth and repeated the berachah on the piece of cake, as Honey directed him.

When he finished eating, Detective Solomon moved his chair back. He replaced the cigar butt and folded his arms over his ample girth.

"Well, we've got all the local criminals," he said, "but they're not talking."

"What does that mean?" Sara asked.

"We captured a whole gang, and even the *dai low*, but we're still not sure who was the 'elder brother's' contact and with which Tong."

"So?" Judy asked, still not quite grasping Detective Solomon's hints.

"Well," Detective Solomon continued, "that still puts you two girls in danger."

I began to shiver as I imagined reliving Menachem's recent adventures.

We all exchanged glances of horror. I began to suspect a gang member spying through every window pane.

"Maybe," I hesitantly suggested, "maybe we can let out the word, through Chaim, that we don't have the jewel in our possession."

"And then how will the jewel get to the East Coast?" Menachem asked.

I saw Sara's face light up with a smile.

"Uh-oh," I said under my breath.

"Let's just ship the jewel back to the East in a bottle of wine!" she laughingly suggested.

Detective Solomon let his chair fall with a bang.

"Hey," he said to us. "You've got a head on your shoulders. Ever think of becoming a detective?"

Everyone laughed, while I felt my face becoming redder and redder.

"You're in technicolor," Menachem teased.

That only caused me to become more embarrassed.

Everyone laughed again, and when the noise quieted down a little, Detective Solomon continued.

"I think you're safe from any of the local gangs," he said. "Those who participated in the kidnapping have been rounded up. The local representative from the Tong has not come forward for the release of his thugs. That in itself is an unusual development. Obviously, they don't want to admit any connection with the gang and the kidnapping.

"But the East Coast connection, though," Detective Solomon continued, "is another story. Those are different gang members and a different Tong. I've got to work on another plan."

There I was, just beginning to relax and enjoy myself, and Detective Solomon came along to reveal the news that there would probably be another group of criminals waiting to surprise us on the East Coast. I gave an involuntary shiver.

Sara saw my reaction and tried to calm me down.

"Don't worry," she tried to reassure me. "Detective Solomon's friends will constantly be protecting us."

With these words, the two detectives began to prepare themselves for departure.

"When are you girls going back East?" he asked us.

"Well, we're going to be taking them up to see the Redwoods tomorrow," Shoshi explained. "And then they'll be taking tomorrow night's flight back to New Jersey."

"When I develop my plan," Detective Solomon indicated, "I'll get in touch with you. Anyhow, it was nice meeting you two. Have a safe trip back. And remember that we'll be keeping an eye on you until that antique jewel gets into the right hands on the East Coast."

The detectives began nearing the door.

"Detective Solomon," Sara said as she approached him. "Can I ask you a question?"

"Sure," he responded patiently, his hand clutching the door knob.

"Do you ever light that cigar butt?" Sara asked quickly, in one breath.

Detective Solomon nearly swallowed the cigar butt as he slowly opened the front door and started walking down the steps.

The outside lightbulb winked and flickered in the darkness as Detective Solomon turned around to face Sara.

"*What* cigar butt?" he roared.

17

BACK TO NEW JERSEY

We were sitting on the airplane. I couldn't believe the whole week had passed by. All our luggage was stored in the cargo compartment. Barry had handed us a carton of wine as we were leaving.

"There's a different mixture of wines I included," he explained. "Tell your father to drink the Beaujolais soon. That wine was just bottled today, and it's supposed to be drunk while it's still fresh."

We nodded our heads, not understanding a thing about the different types of wines and their tastes. All I knew was that most wines tasted better when they were aged.

Judy had kissed us goodbye, and she was crying.

"I'm sorry this visit wasn't a completely happy one," she said. "You have to come again, and then we won't get involved in a mystery."

When we kissed Honey goodbye, I promised to send her all of my old dolls. They were just sitting in boxes up on the shelf of my closet.

"It was your doll playing," I reminded Honey, "that helped us on the right track to the kidnappers in Chinatown."

It was hard saying goodbye to Menachem. Since I was the youngest in my family, I was beginning to feel almost like he was my kid brother. I had even begun calling him Menachem the Professor. He retaliated by calling me Detective Bracha.

Shoshi, though, gave us the biggest surprise of all.

"Our goodbye," she had said, "is really for a very short time. My mother decided that since I have to leave San Francisco for high school anyhow, I might as well stay with relatives. For my senior year in high school I'll be attending Rivkah Gross Academy High, and I'll be boarding at your house."

It was great news, since we had become very close during the past week.

I could hear the engines beginning to rev up. I took out my siddur to say *tefillas haderech* and began to settle down. I looked around the cabin, expecting to see Detective Wong or Detective Solomon silently protecting us. Nobody looked the part of a detective. I shrugged my shoulders.

Oh well, I thought to myself. *There must be someone*

*official on the airplane with us. I just have to have a little
more bitachon.*

Detective Solomon hadn't returned the jewel to us.

He said he would send it with one of his couriers. I
didn't think that was a wise decision. Those thugs could
overpower anyone. But it at least gave the trip an air of re-
laxation. There was that much less to worry about.

"What are you doing?" I asked Sara.

"Well, I'm glad you asked. Maybe you had better help
me," Sara said.

She was unpacking piles of notes and information bulle-
tins from her carry-on bag. Everything was a mess in her bag,
but Sara always seemed to know exactly where each item was.

"I'm trying to redeem myself," Sara confessed.

I had no idea what she was talking about. As I saw her
sorting all the papers that referred to the physical geography of San Francisco into one pile, I began to suspect what
she had in mind.

"Are you planning on writing a report for World
Geography?" I asked her.

"I figured that maybe if we would hand in some extra-
credit report on the geography of the West, Miss
Grosswald would figure that into our grade..."

"And then that last test mark won't look so bad," I concluded.

"You've got the idea," Sara admitted sheepishly.

"It's a good idea," I agreed. "But maybe we should also
give an oral report. That way, the rest of the class could
benefit, and *everyone's* grade will improve."

"Great idea," Sara admitted.

We spent a good part of the trip sorting out and writing our report.

"I can't wait until we get our pictures back," Sara said.

"My mother has a great place to send the pictures to be developed," I answered. "If we give them to her when we arrive in the morning, she'll be able to bring them back home by noon, right before we go back to school."

"Fantastic," Sara said. "Then we can add it all into our report. Hopefully, Miss Grosswald will allow us to give our report tomorrow."

"Now that we've planned out the day," I said, "I don't know how you feel, but I had better take a nap immediately."

"Well, at least we don't have to be in school until the afternoon," Sara said, yawning.

With those profound words, we both curled up in our small airplane seats. Before we knew it, we were arriving at Newark airport.

The day was overcast, and it looked like it was about to rain. My mother picked us up at the airport. Her plan was to drop us off at our respective houses to sleep, and then she would go to school. She would come home at lunchtime to pick us up for the rest of the school day.

I could hardly keep my eyes open. As I walked through the airport and picked up my luggage, I felt as if I was sleepwalking. The smoggy Eastern air only contributed to the unreality of the situation. I was so befuddled and tired that the whole scene was one of massive confusion.

I sat on the box of wine Barry had given as a gift to my father, while I waited for Sara's luggage to arrive. I must have dozed off, with my chin resting in my hands, when I felt myself practically shoved off my comfortable perch. I looked around in surprise and checked that all my luggage was intact. Vaguely, I saw some kind of commotion taking place near the information counter. Almost immediately, Sara joined me, and we followed my mother to the waiting car.

I tried to concentrate on telling my mother everything, but each time Sara would interrupt me, which was of course very often, I lost my train of thought.

After yawning for perhaps the millionth time, I turned to my mother.

"I'm sorry, Mom," I said. "I know this whole mystery story sounds berserk. But I'm so tired I can't even think straight. As soon as you come home for me at lunchtime, we'll talk. I'll have napped already, and I'll be more awake."

Sara gave all the films to my mother.

"I'll drop off the pictures at the Quikee Photo Store. They promise to have your pictures in an hour," she said. "I hope they'll be ready when I come home for lunch."

Although I had only been away from home for a week, when I arrived in the house, everything looked brand new. I had really had a good time in San Francisco, but I appreciated sleeping in my own bed and being surrounded by my own familiar furnishings.

I slept all morning. As I started to make some sandwiches for lunch, I heard Mom's key turning in the lock. We sat down in the kitchen, and as we ate, I reviewed everything that had happened to us in San Francisco.

Of course, Mom had heard the highlights of the mystery. As things were happening, I had made sure to keep her up to date. But now, as I filled her in on all the details, she realized what we had gone through.

"I'm glad I didn't know the danger you girls were in," she said. "I'm quite sure I would have had you brought home immediately."

I was glad that hadn't happened and we had been able to see the whole mystery through.

"And I'm sure," Mom continued, "that had Tatty realized the danger you were exposed to with this antique jewel, he would have found another way to transport it back East."

"I wonder," I added.

"Yes?" my mother questioned.

"Well, did Tatty receive the jewel yet?" I asked.

"I don't think so," Mom answered. "Tatty hasn't really spoken to me about it at all."

We were right in the middle of the conversation when the telephone rang.

I ran to answer it. Sara was at the other end.

"Good morning, sleeping beauty," she said.

"The same to you," I answered. It's a wonder how flippant you get after a good, long sleep.

"You know," she said seriously. "I've been trying to figure out if Detective Solomon sent the jewel with a detective who was on our flight."

"I don't know," I answered. "I also can't figure that out. But, *baruch Hashem*, nobody tried to kidnap us, and we're back home safe and sound."

"Yeah," Sara added. "It's funny that the Eastern gangs

didn't even suspect us of carrying the jewel. Nobody tried to kidnap us, or even to hijack any of our luggage."

Just as Sara was making that statement, a memory began to jiggle in my mind.

"Wait a minute," I said excitedly. "I think you're wrong!"

"What do you mean?" Sara asked.

"Think back to the airport," I commanded.

We had been so tired when we'd arrived at Newark airport early in the morning, the whole scene had seemed enveloped in a fog.

"I don't remember anything unusual," Sara began to say. "Hey, wait. Do you mean the fuss that very heavy man with the tiny feet was making?"

"Yeah," I reminded her. "Did you happen to hear what he was making so much noise about?"

"Hey," Sara excitedly replied. "Wasn't he angry about a carton of wine that was shipped from a Sonoma winery and hadn't arrived?"

"Think a little more," I commanded again. "Wasn't he protesting *after* he tried to pick up *our* carton of wine?"

"That's right!" Sara shouted excitedly into the phone. "But he couldn't get it because *you were sitting on the carton!*"

"I wonder why he was interested in the wine..." I said as I let my voice trail off. I sat thinking that thought over again, holding the telephone, not even realizing Sara had hung up.

A few minutes passed by as I sat in the same position on the floor, cross-legged, cradling the dead phone in my hand. Suddenly, there was a knock on the door.

I went to the door to open it, kind of in a dreamlike state. It was only Sara standing at the door.

"You missed me already," I greeted her sarcastically.

Sara shrugged her shoulders and answered. "I think I figured out where Detective Solomon hid the jewel for your father," she said.

"You can't wait until the *se'udas hoda'ah* tonight to ask him?" I questioned teasingly.

Together we approached the still-sealed box of wine.

"Sorry," Sara said. "But I'm sure the jewel was hidden in this carton of wine. I'd like to discover it before your father shows it to us. I'm sure *we* were the couriers Detective Solomon was referring to." She paused for breath, then continued, "Okay, let's do this scientifically."

"And how do we accomplish that?" I asked.

"We open the box very slowly and search every inch very carefully."

We did just that — not once, not twice, but three times.

First we inspected the carton itself.

There was no glittering jewel.

Then we inspected the extra cushioning Barry had wrapped each bottle in.

There was no glittering jewel.

We then inspected the overall packaging material. It was the soft plastic that had loads and loads of plastic bubbles. Very carefully we inspected each plastic bubble to see if the glittering jewel was sealed inside.

No glittering jewel.

We then reinspected each plastic bubble, in case we had missed one.

There was still no trace of a glittering jewel.

We even felt the surface of each bottle. Perhaps the glittering jewel was sealed under a label.

There was no glittering jewel.

Sara picked up each bottle of wine and lifted it up to the light. Maybe they had hidden the glittering jewel in the wine itself.

But no, there was no glittering jewel.

"I give up." I sat back on the floor, defeated.

"Maybe we really weren't the couriers," Sara admitted in defeat.

We restuffed the box of wine and disposed of all the extra packaging paper, when my mother walked into the room.

"Surprise!" she said, and handed a big paper bag over to us.

"Sorry. I completely forgot about giving them to you when I walked through the door. Hurry up, though. I've got to get back to school...and so do you!"

"The pictures!" Sara and I screamed together as we pounced upon my mother.

We quickly sifted through the pictures and explained all the scenes to my mother.

"And this is nothing," I said. "In real life, it's just stupendous!"

We chose the pictures that were appropriate for our report and tacked them on to the papers we had worked on on the plane.

"I sure hope Miss Grosswald likes what we've done," Sara said.

18

BACK TO SCHOOL

We got to school after lunch and were immediately surrounded by all our friends.

"You two girls," Naomi said, "always have the most exciting times."

"Yeah," Tova agreed. "I've been all over the world, in Mexico and in Israel, and I *never* solved a mystery, or was even involved in one."

Sara was excitedly telling everyone all the details of our encounters with the criminals and kidnappers. I was content to stand at the side and listen to what she was saying, until Miriam cornered me.

"Is what Sara saying *really* true?" she questioned. "Or is she exaggerating the story?"

The attention was then shifted to me. I began to blush.

"Yes," I agreed. "Everything Sara said really happened to us."

"Was it scary?" Naomi asked.

I answered "yes" as Sara answered "no."

Everyone laughed. That response had been very typical of our personalities. I was always afraid, and even though sometimes Sara was too, she would never admit to it.

Riiiing!

The bell to start our afternoon classes had rung.

That day, when it came time for our World Geography class, Sara and I gave our oral report. It was received by the class and by Miss Grosswald with great interest. Sara and I each received an A for the extra-credit report. And anyone who would write up a brief summary of our oral report would also receive extra credit.

We had definitely redeemed ourselves from our erev Pesach mischief-making caper.

A surprise awaited us during the next period. Our *Ivris* teacher was absent, and Rabbi Efram substituted for her.

It wasn't in character for Rabbi Efram to acknowledge that we had been absent from a week of classes. So when Rabbi Efram began questioning us about our trip to San Francisco, *in the middle of class*, we were astounded. But we answered his questions.

"I am aware that you have brought home pictures of the scenery on the West Coast," Rabbi Efram commented. "What did you learn from this?"

We explained how every time we had seen some spectacular scenery we had really appreciated the greatness of Hashem.

I know the answer sounded very studious and perhaps a little artificial. But it really expressed our true emotions. Seeing the magnificent scenery had really emphasized for us the literal greatness of Hashem.

"And what about your experience at the winery," Rabbi Efram continued. "Did you learn anything there?"

"Well, besides learning how wine is made," Sara said about our tour of the winery, "I realized how careful you have to be when making kosher wine. All you need is one innocent non-Jew to decide to inspect a wine barrel. It would cause the wine to be unfit for Jews to drink."

Rabbi Efram nodded his head.

"Do you see?" he told the class. "Everything we do and every place we go has a lesson for us to learn.

"These two girls went to San Francisco for a bar mitzvah. They could have come home with exciting talk about the bar mitzvah — and only about the bar mitzvah. But instead, there are great Torah lessons they have also learned."

Rabbi Efram was just about to change the subject and go on to the scheduled lesson, when I raised my hand shyly.

"Yes, Bracha," he acknowledged me.

"Well, I learned something else, too," I said, as I took a deep breath. I didn't want this to sound too corny, but I continued. "I learned to be happy where I am."

Everyone looked at me suspiciously. The whole class would have given anything to live outside of Pineville, in some exotic area.

"I'm glad to be where I am," I repeated. "It's so hard to be a *frum* Jew outside of a yeshivah community. We don't even realize how lucky we are.

"We all dress in a *tzniusdik* manner. We almost don't even realize how the rest of the world looks or acts, because among ourselves we all act and look the same. Take my cousin Shoshi. She's one of the few girls in her neighborhood who wears long sleeves."

"And your cousin, Menachem," Sara interrupted. "If it wasn't for him, how many of his friends would be wearing a yarmulke and tzitzis today?"

As Sara said these words, I knew there was one more thing I had wanted to say.

"And, yes, look at Menachem," I repeated. "*He's* a real example of someone who knows how to live the life of a *frum* Jew against all odds. If he would have been even a little bit assimilated, we would never have been able to discern him from the kidnappers."

That last statement of mine caused a buzz in the classroom.

"I mean," I explained, "Menachem is always proud to be a Jew. He wears his yarmulke and tzitzis with pride. The only way we were able to tell Menachem was being dragged into the Chinese restaurant was because he was wearing his yarmulke. That was his badge of pride. I learned from my experience with Menachem and the mystery never to try to blend in. I learned to stand up and be proud to be a Jew."

Rabbi Efram nodded his head, and we finally got down to learning some *Ivris*.

19

A VERY SPARKLING WINE

It was finally time for the *seudas hoda'ah*. I quickly finished setting the table in the dining room. There were corn chips and potato chips and lots of soda and nosh around.

Mom was in the kitchen with Rina's mother. They were putting the finishing touches on the cold cuts and the salads they were preparing. Sara's family was coming over to help celebrate our safe return from California. We were going to have a grand party.

Tatty is a connoisseur when it comes to wine, and he was anxiously awaiting the opportunity to taste some of Barry's private stock. Of course, the Beaujolais, which was supposed to be drunk while fresh, was the first bottle that Tatty was going to open.

I laughed to myself when I thought of Tatty's interest in wine. Barry, also, had this unusual involvement with the chemistry and finesse of different wines. It must have something to do with the Friedman blood, I chuckled to myself, even if it certainly seemed to be skipping my generation.

Ding-dong.

It was the front doorbell. The Goodman family entered, and the party immediately began. Who could just sit around after a dozen new people arrived at once?

I was exaggerating, since not all the Goodmans were in Pineville. Channie, Sara's oldest sister, was in a seminary in Eretz Yisrael, and her three oldest brothers were away at yeshivah. But compared to my quiet little family, the Goodmans always give off a party spirit.

We were noshing and really enjoying ourselves, when Tatty banged on the table for quiet.

"Okay, everyone," he said. "Now comes the highlight of our party. Now everyone will get a chance to have a sip of Barry Friedman's best.

"But not only that," Tatty mischievously teased Sara and me. "You will also get to see the fruits of your labors."

Tatty is always punning, and so Sara and I exchanged tolerant glances.

As Tatty proceeded to whip out a corkscrew, and with a grand flourish, to dramatically open the bottle of wine, I began to suspect what Tatty was hinting at.

Tatty began to slowly twist the corkscrew.

Nothing happened.

"What's the matter?" Mom asked.

"Do you need some help?" Rabbi Goodman offered to assist.

"Not really," Tatty said, as he continued to try to force the corkscrew through the cork.

"Oh, oh," Mom said.

"Yep," Tatty answered, "I really goofed it up now."

But as Tatty said these words, I saw him exchange a look with Mom.

Tatty started taking the bits of cork off, as the cork slowly disintegrated in front of our eyes. Finally, he triumphantly uncorked the bottle, and started pouring a little wine out for all the adults.

They all said the berachah, took a sip, and then said *l'chaim*.

Meanwhile, as the adults were remarking about the goodness of the wine, and the other children were busy drinking soda and eating the nosh, Tatty took the cork apart completely. As he did so, he began to unearth something.

It was true. We really *had* been the couriers. Detective Solomon — and I'm sure with Barry's expertise — had buried the precious jewel in an oversized cork.

"Why didn't you tell us we were carrying the jewel?" I asked Tatty accusingly.

"Would you have been relaxed and at ease?" Tatty countered back.

Sheepishly, Sara and I exchanged glances, definitely knowing our response.

Mrs. Goodman began gathering her family together.

Tatty played with the small, precious antique jewel, investigating it.

"Well, girls," Tatty said, as he playfully fingered the jewel, "would you like to take a closer look at the gem that was the cause of so much activity?"

Sara and I were given the jewel to inspect. It was really very beautiful. It was a smooth, oval jade encircled with bright, glittering diamonds. The whole piece was set in gold, with a small loop on the top for a chain.

I handed the jewel back to Tatty, puzzled as to why a smile was still playing at the corner of his mouth.

"I don't know," Tatty commented, "if I would hire you to be my detectives."

I knew Tatty was teasing. Tatty took his jeweler's magnifying glass from his pocket and then handed the jewel and the magnifying glass back to me.

"Now," Tatty said, "maybe you had better inspect this jewel a little more carefully."

Sara looked at the jewel first, but she did so in a very hurried and haphazard fashion. I inspected the jewel a lot more carefully."

"Is that writing on the back?" I questioned my father.

When I had first been given the jewel, the back hadn't seemed smooth to the touch. I had assumed there were scratches on the setting, since it was an antique and had gone through many hands. Now, however, when I was given the opportunity to inspect the jewel with a special jeweler's magnifying glass, I was able to see that the scratches were really writing.

"Can you read it?" Tatty asked me.

"It's Hebrew!" I exclaimed in wonder, and began to read. "'*Pidyon Shevuyim*, France — 5641. Italy — 5678. Poland — 5704.' I don't understand."

I looked at my father questioningly.

"You see," Tatty explained, "this jewel isn't only a precious gem. It has a history that is special to the Friedman family. Our family has exchanged this jewel as a bribe to officials so that Jewish individuals could be freed from prisons.

"It was used as a bribe in private dealings, but even during the Second World War it was in a package to save Jews from the concentration camps. After each release, we were fortunate to receive this jewel back. Then we would engrave the date and the place of the incident on the back."

Tatty paused, and with a lowered voice he nodded toward Rina, who was sitting on the side of the room talking to her parents.

"We can now add," Tatty said, "a new date to this historical piece. USSR — 5749.

"This jewel was used to bribe the officials to help release Rina and Shira," Tatty added at our questioning glances. "We traced it to China, and through certain contacts, we were able to get the jewel to the States."

Tatty then added, "I overpaid its value to get it back."

"Is that why the Chinese gangs got involved?" Sara asked.

"Well, kind of," Tatty admitted. "You see, when I spoke to my contact in Chinatown about the jewel's value, I had to explain the sentimental value the jewel held. I didn't know this then, but according to Detective Wong, the Chinese hold great store in the 'charm' of an object. With its history, this jewel became a valued talisman.

"It became something the Chinese Tong head wished to possess for its good luck," Tatty continued. "That was why he had the two gangs, the Black Vultures and the Red Vultures, vying to steal the jewel. But I must admit that I never realized how much danger I would be putting you in when I asked Barry to give it to you to bring back here."

"So are we still in danger?" I asked nervously.

Tatty laughed.

"No, my child," he said. "Once the jewel reached my hands, the game was over. In their interpretation, the jewel was only available to them during transport. Since I paid for the jewel, once it's in my hands the transaction is completed.

"It's remarkable," he added, "how much trouble, how much crime, was caused by this little piece of imperial jade and a couple of diamonds."

As Tatty stood, musing about the jewel, I sat and observed the scene.

Tatty was showing the jewel to Mom.

Rabbi and Mrs. Goodman were piling their family into the station wagon.

Sara was chewing on some cold cuts.

Rina and her parents were sitting in the corner, speaking animatedly in Russian.

My ninth grade year at Rivka Gross Academy High School was almost over. I had made many new friends and had experienced many exciting adventures. I looked fondly at Sara. We did seem to be a dynamic duo together. Wherever we went, adventure and mystery seemed to greet us.

Oh well, I wondered silently to myself. *I wonder what kind of quiet summer this is going to turn out to be.*

Or would it perhaps bring us our next adventure as the girls of Rivkah Gross Academy High?

ACKNOWLEDGMENTS

Dear Readers,

My husband and I were touring the west coast of the United States, and we were awed by its natural beauty. What a picturesque world Hashem created! As an author, I tried to figure out how I could use this beautiful scenery as a setting in one my books. And that's how *The Golden Gate* was born.

I wanted to incorporate the ancient legend of there being Jewish Asians, and that was where my research of Aunt Ahuvah began. There actually was a group of Yidden who moved to China and assimilated with non-Jews, but many kept their Jewish identity by making sure that only the Jewish females intermarried. Since Yiddishkeit is determined by the religion of the mother, all those born of Jewish mothers remained Jewish. Because, however, they intermarried with Chinese males, many had Chinese features.

✻ ✻ ✻

I remember my school days, and although I have to con-
fess that I actually learned...I also had a lot of fun. But the
highlights of my days were my extracurricular activities.
And for this I have to give my grateful thanks and apprecia-
tion to my esteemed high school principal, Rabbi Ephraim
Oratz, *alav hashalom*. He graced the halls of BYA High
School with a softness and sincerity that touched each
girl's heart, and yet he also disciplined with love and respect for each girl's feelings.

My father, Moshe Mordechai Stavsky, *a"h*, worked in
numerous businesses throughout his life. He was not a
teacher or a rebbe. But his love for learning, his precise-
ness with always davening with a minyan, was a *chinuch*
of the highest order. My mother, Chana Stavsky, *a"h*,
was a true partner. Her love for her children and students
was renowned. She began as a secretary to Rabbi Oratz,
and then moved up the *chinuch* ladder until she partnered
with Rebbetzin Twersky to open up Tomer Devorah High
School. There she embedded a love for Yiddishkeit while
administrating the teachers in the secular skills needed to
live and work in our American world.

My husband, Meir, was once offered a job working with
youth in Eretz Yisrael. It was always our dream to move
there, but when faced with this decision, my husband de-
clined. He felt that Hashem had given him the talent of
teaching American out-of-town youth, and as he became
a rebbe in Dallas, Phoenix, and Boston, he had a strong
influence on nurturing the Torah souls of these precious
children.

❋ ❋ ❋

I would like to thank my children and their spouses, Layah, Shayndy and Lazer, Malkie and Yossie, Mordy and Miriam, Bayla and Yankie, Avrami and Ayala, Avigayil, Michal, Rivky and Boruch, and Shulamis. Your focus on transferring your Torah values to the next generation makes me proud.

And to my grandchildren: Rivky and Menachem Markowitz, Yehudah Mandelbaum, Aliza and Menachem Gringras; Rivka, Raizel, and Devora Abrahamson; Chaim Horowitz, Rikki and Sholom Hochman, Bracha, Adina, Shiri, and Eli Horowitz; Moshe Leib, Yehudis, Dovid, Yitzchok, and Shmuel Gross; Avrami Hersh, Rivky and Elchonon Gartenhaus, Esti, Eli, and Shimi Hersh; Faigy, Mordechai, Shoshana, Tehila, Miri, Chani, and Gitty Gross; Racheli, Ezzy, and Penina Bendkowski; and Chana and Moshe Bernstein.

And to the new generation, Moshe Gringras and Moshe Hochman. You are the best critics. Keep on reading and discovering new worlds. (And see! All your names are in this book!)

I would like to thank the Eibeshter for guiding my thoughts and words in creating novels of interest for young adults. Hashem runs the world, and I am happy to do His bidding.

I would be remiss if I did not mention CIS Publications, the venue where *The Golden Gate* first appeared. I am privileged that Menucha Publishers selected my book as an addition to their reading list.

I daven that at this time of publication, Covid-19 will

be a memory of the past, and Mashiach Tzidkeinu will be lighting a new pathway of *chinuch* in our schools.

Sukey Gross

Don't miss Sukey Gross's first two books about the girls from Rivkah Gross Academy!

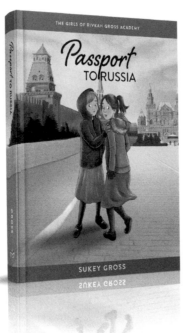

Passport TO RUSSIA

On her very first day of ninth grade, Bracha meets Sara, a mischievous classmate who quickly draws her into her exploits. The two girls jump right into the mystery of the local candy store owners. What secret lies behind their sad and angry faces?

Bracha and Sara are thrilled to be invited on the adventure of a lifetime...a visit to the USSR, where they'll meet Jews trapped behind the Iron Curtain.

Meet Bracha, Sara, and their friends in this lively, page-turning book, now back in print!

THE Secret DIARY

A snowy Shabbaton, a hidden diary, and a lost daughter...

Bracha, Sara, and their classmates are thrilled to be invited to an inter-school Shabbaton in Mount Airy, Pennsylvania. As soon as they arrive, they're plunged into the mystery of the wealthy man who left so much of his fortune to the local community. Who was he, and why did his daughter vanish without a trace? And will the startling discovery of a secret diary lead them to the poignant answers?

Join the girls and their friends in this exciting story, now back in print!

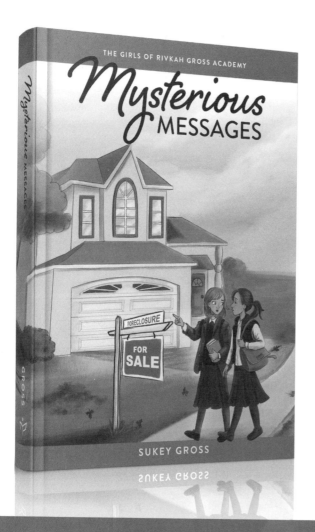

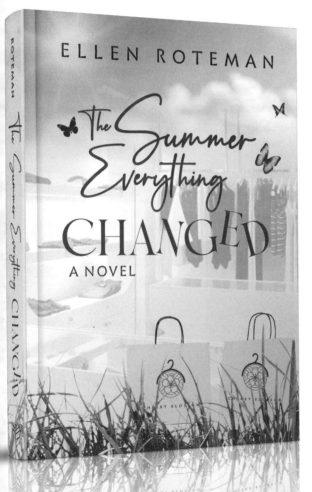